Hollows of the Nox

by Matthew E. Nordin

Shadows of Eleanor

book one

Matthew Nordin

This is a work of fiction. All of the characters, organizations, and events portrayed in his novel are either products of the author's imagination or are used fictitiously.

Cover art by Chris Ralston of R10 Creations
https://www.patreon.com/ChrisRalston

HOLLOWS OF THE NOX / Shadows of Eleanor, book 1
ISBN: 978-0-578-47509-7

for those who understand the power of words

1

Sagging shelves of books and the scent of ancient paper welcomed Eldritch to his familiar shop. The planting season was over, and he could finally enjoy the myriad of stories and languages few had the privilege to read. The two-story building held more writings than any place within a hundred miles of his village. How the old building held it all without falling over was beyond him.

Although more of a library, the fantastic collection of books was available to buy or trade. The locals of Raikrune stopped in for an occasional herbal drink while the real customers were the wanderers. The pages of things forgotten lured strange visitors. People from all races of the known world stopped in to browse the rare collection.

Luckily for the community, the travelers liked to buy some of the local crops as well. This was likely the main reason why the shop remained in Raikrune. The rest of the town did not share Eldritch's passion for books.

"Too much of that reading is bad for you," Sayeh quipped from over Eldritch's shoulder. "Someday I'll have to charge you for all your time in here."

Although Sayeh was the only other person in the building, Eldritch jerked back in the wooden chair. It cracked and popped from age and misuse.

He froze.

It would not be the first time one of the decrepit chairs broke from under him, even though his father teased him about his petite frame and ordinary looks. In fact, none of the other locals gave him a second glance.

Except for Sayeh, who stared at him. The young caretaker of the shop looked different from the last time he saw her—an allure he hadn't noticed when they were children.

She pointed at a map on the page he was studying.

"My father tells me to keep your head in your own work and not in the noses of others," she said. "Or something like that.

From what I can tell, it's what all those foreign languages are about."

"I believe they say, you should not put your nose in other people's business. Or books." Eldritch turned and studied Sayeh's face. She kept her youthful smile, but her lips were fuller. He didn't care if she read any of the books, as long as she enjoyed hovering near him.

"Well, whose ever nose it is, why are you so interested in other people's tales when there are good things here?" She brushed her hair back and leaned against the table. It too creaked from the age of the soft wood.

"Where else could I learn about the unknown horrors of the deep ocean, or the merchants who trade with the malevolent elves, or delight in the whimsical and elusive magic of the fae? I wish I lived closer to the border town." Eldritch stopped to take a breath, imagining himself wandering along the edge of the forbidden fairy forest.

There was one soul who managed to get close to the hidden entrance. The one whose journal laid before him written in a language few could understand. The one Sayeh rested her arm on with her jaw slightly opened.

Her blank expression brought him a sense of bliss. Being born in Autumn, she appeared to radiate the crisp season. He found himself staring into her amber eyes.

"Can I get you something to drink at least?" She winked.

Eldritch's cheeks grew warm. He tried to speak but feared his words would fall from his lips like a bumbling drunkard. The poetry he'd read escaped his speech with each look she gave him, a mesmerizing beauty.

"Whatever is nearby, thank you," he managed to sputter.

She turned to the kegs lining the bar area. Although the locals preferred the tavern for drinks, travelers would often find themselves lingering among the extravagant collection of books in the shop. Most browsed through and did not make any purchases, but they did buy Sayeh's herbal drinks. Her mother had taught her a recipe for boiling different leaves to create unique and invigorating blends. Sayeh expanded on those for her own flavors, with some help from Eldritch.

"This first one's on me." Sayeh returned with a full mug. "What are you learning about today?"

"It's the fairies," Eldritch said. "The fae folk, I mean. They live north and west of us, before the sea. Their realm is guarded by a mysterious barrier none have been able to pass."

"Well, if no one's been in there, how do they know about them?" Sayeh set the drink in front of him.

The chair across from him squeaked loudly as she sat down. She giggled from the noise before resting her arms on the table. Eldritch tried to hold back a laugh but the grin plastered across his face gave him away.

"The fairies?" She questioned again. "How does anyone know about them?"

"They trade with the settlers on the border towns." He glanced at the book. "It's rare when they come. Sometimes not for years between visits. But they love showing their tricks and telling stories to the humans. . . us, I mean. This book is written by one who tried to sneak inside."

"Did he make it in?" She leaned closer to the book.

"He disguised himself with magic and followed a fairy right to the edge of their forest. But something made him turn away."

"Did the fairy put a spell on him?"

"It's unclear. It says he was blinded and lost consciousness, then he woke up farther away from the forest than he had been. A feeling of lost hope overtook him. Something dire. It invaded his thoughts, and he fled back to Caetheal and never ventured there again."

"Does it say anything else about the fairies?" Sayeh picked up another book on the table and flipped through it.

"Yes. I believe there are deeper secrets I have yet to understand." Eldritch looked out the window. The emptiness of the road mirrored his heart, it longed to be filled with the adventure and magic he'd read about. "I must discover the hidden beauty and worlds beyond the ink of these pages." He promised himself.

"I like the ones with the funny looking creatures in them." Sayeh set the book down and leaned back with her arms crossed.

"Those are an additive to a book's real power."

"I'd like to have that power too, I think." Sayeh's eyes widened. "I mean, I hear a lot from the travelers. People's lips loosen with the right drink. You're lucky I haven't used any on you, yet."

Eldritch inspected the drink in front of him. Everything looked normal.

He took a careful sip of the sweet herbal mixture. It tasted of sap and strawberries.

"Would you like me to teach you the languages of these older books?"

"What a wonderful idea!" She clapped her hands together. The movement caused the chair to crack, and one of the legs broke free. Sayeh and the chair crashed to the ground. She started laughing hysterically on the floor.

"Maybe I should teach you how to sit properly in a chair first." Eldritch laughed with her and held out a hand.

She grabbed it and almost pulled him down. The sweet smell of jasmine and vanilla floated up from her dress as it brushed across his leg.

Something jingled from inside the fabric.

"What was that?" Eldritch said after Sayeh steadied herself.

"Sorry, I almost forgot." She plopped a bag of coins on the table. "I need to get this counted before my mother comes to close up. You don't mind, do you?"

Before he could answer, the door swung open.

A man shambled in with the smell of a long and unpleasant journey, not the typical customer for the shop. A couple of empty bottles clanked about his belt. He looked around and found a seat at the nearest table.

"Are you sure you're not looking for the alehouse, sir?" Sayeh asked, but the man leaned back into the chair and shook his head.

"If you're not interested in books or ale, I can make you an herbal drink."

"That'll do," the stranger said while keeping his eyes on Sayeh.

"Where have you traveled from, friend?" Eldritch walked over with his chest out, trying to mask his pale and scrawny features. The way the man stared at Sayeh was unsettling. "Can I help you find a book to your liking?"

"Just passing through is all." The man gazed hard at Eldritch. He turned back to Sayeh who had returned. "A quiet shop is what I've been needing."

"Here you are," she said setting the bottle at his table. "Feel free to grab a book you like but be sure to put it back unless you are looking to purchase it."

Sayeh walked past the man and faced Eldritch with a look he couldn't read. The way she smiled at him and her intoxicating perfume were different than when they were growing up together.

Her smile left her face as she was jerked away from Eldritch. She stumbled back. The man wrapped his bulky arm around her waist.

Eldritch lurched forward, but a dagger was pointed toward him from the man's other hand.

"Easy lad." The man tightened his arm around Sayeh's waist. She stopped struggling as he held the dagger to her neck. "There's no need for anyone to get hurt. I see one bag of coins. Where's the rest?"

Eldritch's mind spun with confusion. He hated feeling powerless but knew he couldn't attempt to overpower the man without Sayeh getting hurt. He looked away toward the door.

"Don't think of going anywhere," the stranger said to Eldritch. "We don't want anything bad happening to such a pretty wench, do we? Sit back in the chair."

The man pulled out a rope. Eldritch couldn't stop staring at it. Something about that rope. There was nothing peculiar about it, only that it would be used to confine him.

"Did you not hear me, boy?" The man loomed closer to him with Sayeh in his grasp. She was shaking. "I said sit down."

The man's words traveled past him as if spoken to someone else far away. The room seemed to spin and his vision blurred as if he were looking at everything from underwater. A new presence lurked along the back recesses of his mind, trying to get his attention.

"You see it?" A voice trailed inside hiss mind, like a breeze blowing by. *"Do you see it? The words are there. You know what they are."*

He peered from the corner of his eye to who or what spoke to him. The unseen voice used an ancient tongue, the old language he had read but never heard.

Eldritch trembled from his racing heart and looked again at the man. Although the stranger held the rope, he did not control it. He did not control the dagger, or Sayeh, or even his mind.

"Do you see me?" Eldritch's words formed deep within an unknown part of his mind before they left his lips. He watched a force wrapping around the man's brain, like the rope in his hands. "You see me. See how you are powerless before me."

The dagger crashed to the ground.

Sayeh pushed away from the man who had dropped the dagger and the rope. He pulled the hair at his temples and knocked over his drink, letting out a loud yell as he fled into the streets.

Liquid soaked into the rotten wood where the stranger once sat. The sound of it dripping on the floor muffled the other noises around the shop.

"Eldritch? What happened? Are you okay?" Sayeh shook him. "Eldritch?"

"Yes." Fatigue filled his words. "He won't come here again. I made sure of that. What about you? Are you okay?"

"I think so." She grabbed his hand. They were softer than he expected. "What was that? You were speaking in some language I've never heard anyone speak before. It was frightening. But it terrified that troll of a man."

"I had to scare him off," Eldritch said. "If you need to go home, I'll clean up the mess."

"You don't need to trouble yourself with that." She pulled him closer. "Perhaps you could stay longer though?"

"It's late." His heart pounded faster. "My parents may start to worry. I believe your mother is coming soon to help you close."

"Yes." Sayeh frowned and looked out the window. "I'll clean the spill before she gets here. Thank you, Eldritch."

"I'm sorry if I scared you with those words." Eldritch tried to remember what he had actually said to the man.

"You'll have to teach me how to speak with such a fearsome voice and the old language. I am eager to learn everything you know."

She gave him that smile again. He nodded as all his other thoughts escaped.

The sun hung low on the horizon when he slipped out of the bookshop. He had to admit, he found Sayeh very attractive, almost enough to forget about his own desires. His parents wanted him to settle down, marry someone from the village, tend the farm, and live a monotonous life. Of course, having the books in the shop at his disposal would be convenient, but he wanted to leave—when the time was right.

There was still much to learn from the mysteries of the books. Something called to him, deep within them. The words spoke to him, spoke through him. He needed to listen to their power.

2

"You came back." Sayeh dropped the book she was about to shelve and sprang to greet Eldritch at the door. "It's been over a week. I thought something may have happened at the farm."

"All is well there," Eldritch said. "I had to help my parents finish planting. It will be best to stay inside with the days getting hotter."

"Are you ready to teach me?" Her smile made him feel warmer than the temperature outside.

Sayeh's complexion should have been lighter compared to those in the fields since she spent most of her time inside, but the layers of unwashed dirt and ink smears created a creamy tan.

"My grandfather taught me to never fear the power of a good book," Eldritch said. "The most simple tome can hold secrets beyond what we can fathom. The older, the better."

"You told me he was blind though. How could he teach you to read?"

"He taught me from what he had learned when he could see, and when his vision failed, he could make out most of the shapes."

Eldritch took a deep breath. His grandfather passed away too suddenly. Although mostly blind, he had the ability to unlock the phrases and symbols of other languages, finding the true meaning of words. It was almost like the books spoke to him in some way beyond sight. The handful of books he memorized had distinct textures on the covers. It was like he could feel the markings on the paper as well.

By teaching another, Eldritch hoped to learn more of the magic his grandfather taught. If he could focus on teaching and not on Sayeh's smile.

"Eldritch?" She waved a hand in front of him. "Are you going to teach me today?"

"Oh yes." He tried to shake off his thoughts and looked away. "If you want to grab us drinks, I'll get the books."

Hollows of the Nox

Days passed as Eldritch taught Sayeh his favorite stories. He first opened the simpler ones of pirating on the seas, assuming she heard such tales from travelers stopping by the bookshop.

In fact, she picked up on them too quickly, like she was faking her naivety for a way to spend more time with him. Of course, he didn't mind spending more time with her. He shivered from the thought of being closer to her.

No, that wasn't it. Something else was reaching into his mind.

"She is keeping you from true power," a voice, not his own, whispered inside his thoughts. *"A waste of time."*

Eldritch stood and looked around the room. No one other than Sayeh.

"Is everything all right?" She asked and raised an eyebrow.

"Yes, sorry, it was nothing." It had to be the wind making noises, or he must have imagined it. Yet the words the voice said left a chill in his chest that wouldn't go away. "Let's get back to the story of the pirate. Do you understand it?"

"Very much and I like it too. Who knew there were elves on the seas? I'd always seen them as pleasant and polite whenever they stopped by here."

"One must have had his ears pulled a little too much growing up." Eldritch laughed to shake off the tension.

Sayeh grabbed her ears and stuck her tongue out at Eldritch.

"Careful not to pull too hard, you might become a pirate too." Eldritch leaned forward and stuck his hands behind his ears. He should have felt foolish, but she enjoyed everything he did. It made him more nervous.

"You would make a great elven pirate," Sayeh said. "Sailing across the deep seas to the fairy lands, but not to good fae, to the dangerous ones who would try to capture you. But you'd fight them off with your clever words and skill."

"She knows," the voice whispered again. *"Ask her. You want to learn more about the dark fae."*

The voice breathed in his ear the way his grandfather would read into the books.

"Can you tell me some of the stories you know of the fae?" Eldritch stammered.

"I don't know if I'd be much help." She blushed and looked at her feet. "I'm sure you know more than I do from those books you read. You study them all day."

"Yes, but you mentioned something about dark fairies. I have not read anything about those creatures. Do they live in the deep waters or another island somewhere?"

"Oh no, not at all." Sayeh moved back in her chair and flopped her leg upon the table to restring her boot lace. "They live in the forest too. Well, one of the travelers said so. He travels through the border towns a lot and has even seen some of the dark fae."

Eldritch tried not to stare at her soft leg. It strained the border of her dress and lifted the hem of it. He swallowed hard, attempting to keep his heart from beating out of his chest. "What else did he say?"

"They're like us, they have good ones and bad ones. There is a balance in the forest, but the bad ones never come out or are locked away somewhere." She shrugged. "He didn't say anything else about them. I imagine they sneak out of the forest and play tricks on the people in town. At least I think that would be more fun to do if I was a dark fairy."

"Interesting concept." Eldritch rubbed his chin. Maybe she knew more than she realized. "So what did this traveler say about the fairies he saw? Were any of those the dark ones?"

17

"He told me their skin was a rainbow of precious jewels and their hair shone like a field of grain on fire. Their eyes were like the twin moons appearing every hundred years. He laughed when I asked how much one of them would be worth."

"Are they traded then?" Eldritch's mind danced with the idea of being able to purchase such a creature. If he were able to get close to one, he could learn of their secret power in the forest.

"He said if anyone could even get within speaking distance of a fairy, it would be a feat all to its own. They like to do business from a distance. Although some have seen them, none have ever been close enough to touch one. I guess it wouldn't be good to try and catch one." Sayeh moved her leg back down and stared at Eldritch. "You're not interested in catching one, are you?"

"I don't know if such a being could be caught. And I can assume the ill fate of one who would try. Has anyone told you anything else about them?"

"All the other stories they told me were similar to the ones you told me from your books." Sayeh's eyes lit up. She reached for the book of fae stories Eldritch kept in his stack. "Do you think the customers who told me the stories could be the writers of those books?"

"I doubt it." Eldritch snatched the book before Sayeh could grab it. "These books were written long before any of us were here. Before your ancestors collected them all."

"I heard one man say that fairies never die and never age. Maybe one of them wrote the book." A certain smile crossed her lips again. "What if someone had a romantic encounter with a fairy?"

Eldritch thought for a moment. He couldn't recall reading anything about a half-fae creature before. "Interesting. I wonder what it would be like if a fairy and human ever—"

"I meant to tell you," Sayeh interrupted. "I'm actually a fairy. We could see what would happen together."

Eldritch's mouth went dry. He let out a nervous laugh and took a drink from his cup. It tasted stronger than usual, dizzying his mind. He put his hand upon Sayeh's. Such intimacy he had read of in stories. The passion of a thousand sonnets sat before him, waiting for him to make the next move.

"Lead her to the back room," the voice said so clearly he jolted up, still holding her hand.

She stood with him.

"Come with me," Eldritch said.

The old building echoed the pulses of his heartbeat. It resounded with his yearning for the private chamber and Sayeh.

The sweat between their hands caused Eldritch to grip her tighter while they twisted through the maze of scattered books and shelves. Sayeh pushed Eldritch into the door as their adrenaline rushed together.

"It's locked," Eldritch said while fumbling with the chains.

"Give me a moment," Sayeh said.

She reached her arm around him and pressed her soft chest into his. Her foot slid between his legs. Eldritch was encapsulated in her sweet perfume. Jasmine and vanilla filled his senses. Her lips hovered near Eldritch's neck.

The chains came loose from the handle and the door opened. Eldritch stepped out of the way. The warped wood and stains of neglect made him wary. Sayeh's alluring scent filled the area and helped him forget his hesitations.

She jumped inside the room with a laugh and twirl.

Her laugh turned into a scream as her legs crashed through the old wood floor.

The rotten boards snagged her dress and cut across her thigh. She hung by the fabric, crying louder while she dangled above a passage below the room.

Her fingernails dug into Eldritch's arm as he grabbed her shoulder.

"My leg!" she shouted.

He tried to pry her from the broken floor. Her leg slid farther into the shards of the board and she shrieked in pain. Eldritch hooked his other arm around her shoulders and caught a glimpse into the chasm below.

Old tomes of books and scrolls shrunk away from the light intruding on them. The streaks of Sayeh's blood soaked into the papers below.

Eldritch lifted with all his might and finally yanked Sayeh free, pulling the board up with her. She crawled farther from the hole and held her leg where the wood had impaled her. Her cries faded to a whimper. More blood spilled from the wound.

"Help me, please." Sayeh gasped and shivered.

Eldritch ripped off his shirt and tied it around her leg.

"Put pressure on this, hold it tight." Eldritch placed her hands over the bandage and sprinted toward the window.

"Help us!" he cried out.

No one was around. No one was ever around when he needed them.

"I need to find someone to help us." Eldritch glared out the window. "This cursed town! Why is no one here?"

"Please, don't leave me," Sayeh begged.

Eldritch rushed to her side. The bandage was soaked through.

"Listen to me," the voice whispered in his ear. *"You can save her. You have the power within."*

A door seemed to unlock in his mind. Memories of stories and spells wove together. A power his grandfather tried to explain.

"What do you mean?" Eldritch cried aloud in frustration. "Who are you?"

"Eldritch. . ." Sayeh whispered.

He looked into Sayeh's eyes. They lingered in a distant direction.

"I'm sorry," he said. "I need to get you help."

He wrapped his arms around her and lifted her from the floor. Strands of wet cloth clung to his arm. His hands slipped on her bloodied skin while he tried to carry her. Her life was fading away.

He continued to call for help, stumbling over the piles of boxes and books.

"They cannot help you," the voice hissed. *"Listen to me!"*

The command caused Eldritch to stumble over a stack of books. He twisted, landing hard on his side to protect Sayeh.

She rolled to the side and made no sound. Her breathing was shallow, and she slipped out of consciousness.

"Listen to me! You have the power to save her."

The voice seemed to be crawling along the base of his skull. It lingered behind his eyesight.

Eldritch clamped his hands around the wound and cried out, "Tell me, please!"

Like fingers running through his hair, the voice moved across his mind. It blurred his vision. His own fingers twitched away from Sayeh as they traced patterns into the bloodied cloth which was once his shirt.

He moaned in strange syllables and patterns he had never read or spoken before. The cloth hardened when he rested his hand back on the wound.

The fingers inside his mind slipped away. His vision returned, and he witnessed the bright red stain continued to darken beyond the crimson until a shell formed around the wound. It resembled a hardened mass of charred wood.

Eldritch rested his ear on Sayeh's chest. Her heartbeat slowly pulsed. She was alive.

He slid his hand from the wound to her side and eased her onto her back. It took more of his strength to move the books out from under her than it had to pull her from the hole. The material around the wound sizzled and smoked.

He pushed himself up from the ground and grabbed some of the cleaning buckets. Although he had helped Sayeh many times with them full of water, a weakness sunk into the fiber of his bones that caused him to carry it with half the amount. Whatever spell he cast, drained him.

He glanced outside once more in hopes of his luck changing.

Still empty.

None of the other houses gave any hints of life inside them. Only the flies trickled in the building from the cracks in the windows.

The strain of the buckets forced Eldritch to stop. He sighed and dragged them closer to Sayeh, pulling out a strip of cloth.

The rags scraped across the crusted wound on her leg like a mop on a dry floor. Scrubbing had no effect. He wiped away the blood from the other parts of her skin. The water, tainted red, stained his pants as he finished cleaning.

He placed his ear to her chest again and listened to her breathing. It continued as before.

A chill pulled him away, and he caught a glimpse of the chamber under the broken floor again in the corner of his eye. A desire to discover what treasures lay hidden in such a place tempted him, but he feared he was already losing his sanity. Something took control of him to save Sayeh, and he wasn't sure how much of it had been from his own understanding of magic.

He placed one arm over her waist and wrapped the other under her head. His joints and muscles ached. Perhaps someone would find them and carry them both to a softer place to rest. Perhaps they would slip together into an endless sleep. Whatever happened, he wanted to be with Sayeh.

Every sense of time slowed to a stop as their hearts beat together. Eldritch took steady breaths as he watched Sayeh. He hoped that if he looked at her long enough, her eyes would open and she would give him that smile again.

He tried to stay awake. He wanted to see her wake up, if she were to wake up again. But an unnatural heaviness on his eyes caused him to slip into a blackness of sleep. A sleep unlike any before.

Eldritch's mind sunk beyond the floor of the shop and into the earth. Past the graves of his ancestors and into the sarcophagus of forgotten books. Books that were meant to be buried and remembered no longer. Ones that bridged the realms of life and death. The realms he now balanced on. Whatever entered his mind and gave him power took something from him that could never be replaced.

His mind swirled in that dark abyss. Visions of his past blinked into existence and vanished into the clouded dream. Phantoms of friends he knew but never got close to put their arms around him to drag him deeper into the sleep.

"Is that really you?" a small voice called through the blackness.

Eldritch tried to focus. The shadows darted in front of his eyes. An image formed of a younger man who looked identical to Eldritch. His face was youthful, but his hair grew long and white. It twisted around his face causing a blur of indistinguishable features. The man could almost be Eldritch's younger brother, if he were alive.

"You can't be here." Eldritch gasped. "You died as an infant. How can you be here?"

"We're always here. Always growing while you diminish." The boy's words were choked as if coughing through smoke and ash. "You created me here. I am and am not. We thrive on your loss."

"But you died, how are you older now?"

"Always growing, filling the void. It is endless. We are endless. The shadows consume all."

"I don't understand, where are you, who are you?" Eldritch tried to turn away, but the image of his brother followed his eyes. "You're not my brother. Let me out!"

He could feel the darkness lifting.

"Eldritch, come back! Come back to me! You found us, now save us." The voice trailed away. He felt his whole body shaking.

"What happened to my leg?" Sayeh's voice called. "Eldritch? Come back to me!"

He forced his eyes open as the strength returned to his body. His mind was dizzy from the hallucination as he turned to Sayeh. She had managed to sit up.

"What did you do to my leg?" she asked.

"Is it okay?" Eldritch checked to see if any blood seeped from around the shell.

"It doesn't hurt. But what the hell is on it? It won't come off."

He wanted to give her an answer but didn't know what to say. He rubbed his forehead and sat up.

"You lost a lot of blood. I had to make something to get it to stop," he explained.

"I thought I was dying." Sayeh pushed on the wrap again, but it remained firm.

Eldritch shifted his weight to support her and helped her to her feet. She stood tentatively on the injured leg.

"That's odd," she said and let out a long breath. "I don't feel any pain at all."

"Are you well enough to walk?" Eldritch said, holding her waist.

"Yes. My leg is a little stiff, but I'm fine." She tried to cover the wound with her tattered dress. "My clothes are ruined. I need to go home. My parents will need to know about the damaged floor, and I should probably lie down for a while."

"Let me help you."

Sayeh held her arm out, and Eldritch slipped his hand under it to give her support. He led her through the fallen books.

Although far from the room now, he felt like something watched him from the shadows. The chasm held some sort of answer to his strange vision.

"What happened to you?" Sayeh asked. "You sounded like you were in a deeper sleep than I was."

"I'm not sure." Eldritch focused on the door ahead of them. "I guess I was up too late reading last night."

The sun cast long shadows upon the town when they stepped out. Its heat hung in the air one final hour before nightfall.

"I'll lock up the shop tonight." Eldritch noticed Sayeh's hesitation to leave the building in such a state.

"Thank you, Eldritch." Sayeh placed her hand on his shoulder and kissed him softly on the lips.

His cheeks flushed. He looked around the streets to see if anyone noticed. The town was empty.

Eldritch held out his arm to help Sayeh home. Even though she said it wasn't painful, she could not move it right and limped through the dusty streets.

"I will see you tomorrow?" Sayeh asked when they reached her house.

"Yes. Of course." He smiled and leaned in to kiss her. A movement at the window made him shrink back.

Sayeh nodded to the house and made a shooing motion with her hands before straightening her hair and dress. He was grateful that he did not have to stay and explain anything to her parents.

Eldritch turned back down the street and smiled to himself before strolling back to the bookshop. A few of the brighter stars decided to make themselves known as the sun blinked its eye on the horizon one last time.

The stale air gave no breeze, and the lingering summer heat made him have no wish for his shirt. He rubbed the back of his head and wondered: What had happened to his shirt? Was it encased within the shell around Sayeh's leg, or did it turn into the shell itself? How was she able to stand and walk after losing that much blood?

He reached the door of the shop and peered inside. The sunlight that once filled it was replaced with cool twilight. Eldritch wanted to search the chamber below the floor. He looked down at his half-clothed and blood-soaked appearance.

"Tomorrow," he muttered under his breath.

He closed the door and used the hidden key Sayeh showed him when they were younger to lock up. If all went as planned, he would be able to get home with enough cover of darkness to put on new clothes before his parents saw him.

A building of clouds on the eastern skies quickened his steps as a storm flashed its warnings of light across the land.

3

The path to town was scattered with broken limbs and shards of crops. Eldritch should have felt sorry for leaving so early in the morning. His parents would have much to clean up without him. Thoughts of the old and mysterious books he caught glimpses of filled his mind as he walked past his family's grove of apple trees.

Branches were broken low and twisted to the ground. It was unlike any storm damage Eldritch witnessed before. Something horrendous hit last night. If not for his study of agriculture, their crops would have perished in the decade-long drought like many of the other farms. With the storm, not many remained.

The dryness of the season brought pests to feast on the juicy leaves. Although his parents tried many methods to cut back their reproducing, they managed to pop up on every tree. Their resilience was admirable.

A breeze passed through the remaining leaves, giving a musty tinge to the air. It tugged at his new clothes and urged him to look closer. Weary branches reached for a rejuvenating touch, a spell which would restore them to their former glory. The answer laid beyond the realms of his mind and those of nature. As he had healed Sayeh's leg, he would mend the trees.

He walked over to the apple tree and took a solemn breath. Pressing his hand on the splintered bark, he focused on the power from before. The tree conveyed a sense of being brittle. He tried to force his will upon it to be strong, but no power flowed through him like before.

He grunted again and pushed at the trunk. It swayed listlessly until one of its apples fell, one not overtaken by worms. Eldritch broke it open to be sure. At least he would have breakfast on his journey to town.

The handle to the bookshop door clicked open as he twisted it before using the key.

He jolted back. He was sure he locked it.

"Come in," Sayeh's voice called on the other side of the door. "I'm sorry I cannot greet you there. Do come in and look around. I can answer your—oh. Eldritch." She smiled and repositioned herself at the table.

"You must be feeling better this morning," Eldritch said looking past her in the direction of the back room. He would have to find a way to get her out of the shop so he could explore the hidden area they had discovered.

"Thank you for fixing that hole up last night. I'm sure it kept you up late."

"What do you mean?" Eldritch raised an eyebrow.

"The hole I almost died in," Sayeh said. Her words trailed away as he pushed through the bookshelves to the back room.

The unchained door swung open with an easy push. The floor that had splintered away the night before was replaced by a slab of boards and scorch marks.

Eldritch knelt down and ran a hand across them. The boards were strong and secure as if placed there for years.

He knocked.

The sound echoed back to him. The secret chamber was sealed off again.

"Tell no one of this," he heard the ghastly whisper again. *"Patience. We have waited, now you must wait."*

The scent of ash and sulfur filled his nose, and his eyes burned as if standing in smoke. He could taste it in the air.

"Eldritch, when you get done in there, I have a favor to ask," Sayeh called.

He breathed in hard and coughed. The room could be visited later. He closed the door behind him and returned to the front table.

"I'm afraid I may need you to help me reorganize and clean." She tapped on her leg being propped up by a chair. "I am still trying to figure out how to move right with this thing on. Do you know how long it needs to stay?"

"I don't think it will be long." He hoped. "But I can help you with the shop until it's healed. As long as you give me time to read."

"Of course." Her eyes sparkled. "I would like to keep hearing the stories as well. I know it is asking a lot of you after you have done so much already."

"I'll tell my family you need extra help when I go back. I'm sure they've probably heard of the accident. You know how rumors spread."

"It may not be so bad." Sayeh bit her lip and looked up innocently at him. "I told my parents I fell on one of these old chairs."

"What about the dressing on your leg?"

"I said that you read something about medicinal herbs to stop the bleeding and they stopped asking questions. I don't know why the thing is stuck on me if it doesn't hurt anymore. I've tried peeling it off, but it won't move."

"It should come off naturally," he tried to assure himself more than her. "I'm so sorry for it being that way. Where would you like me to start cleaning?"

The summer's heat wore on Eldritch's determination to help as he spent more hours reorganizing the books than reading them. The desire to explore the chamber under the floor was almost unbearable. But every time he got the courage, Sayeh would show up.

Until the morning she did not arrive.

Eldritch waited. Evening would be approaching soon, so she must have decided to stay home. He had the entire building to himself.

He looked through the front window and locked the entrance. The once-cluttered path to the back room was free of the books he organized. The wooden floor gave a creek as if in anticipation for its secrets to finally be revealed.

He stood in front of the scorch marks from the hole that had repaired itself. There would have to be another way in. The dirt packed into the floor made any hidden switches or levers impossible to locate. Eldritch struggled to get a fingernail between the cracks of the boards. Whatever force mended the hole made everything else in the room more secure.

The chamber below had to have some sort of magical barrier or protection upon it. A powerful one that kept the room hidden for generations. There had to be a trick to unlock it.

Eldritch retraced the events from the night Sayeh fell through the floor a few more times in his mind. All he could remember was casting the spell on her leg. It could be he somehow fixed both her wound and the hole that was torn open. If so, he needed to wait until Sayeh's leg was free of the shell. The two were likely connected, and he did not want to open the floor and the wound on her leg again. Even though the spell came out of his mouth, he had no idea how long it would take to fully heal.

The rattling of the front door made him run out of the back room.

"Sayeh?" he called.

He heard the door open as if not locked at all. Eldritch hurried to the front, hoping he would not have to explain himself to her.

It was not Sayeh. A large man in a coat that hung to his boots stomped inside.

"You there, young lad," he said in an earthy accent. "I need your help in finding course."

He placed his giant hand upon one of the heaviest chairs and drug it away from the table like a toy. His massive frame could have used two chairs. He sat and stared intently at Eldritch.

Eldritch eyed the chair, ready for it to break under the weight.

"I am not the owner of these books. My friend is ill, so I've been helping when I can," he explained.

"That is no good then." The man leaned back and removed his hat. Although his hair fell down quickly, Eldritch thought he saw the elongated ears of an elf. "I don't suppose you know how to read any of these maps and charts do ya?"

"I do, in fact. I'm probably the only one in this town who enjoys learning about other regions. I've studied most of the areas documented in these books."

"Ah, good on you then." The man crossed his arms over his large belly. "Tell me, what would be the easiest path to Caetheal, the crossing town of the great forest and the harbor?"

"I have the book right next to you with the map."

Adrenaline caused Eldritch to shake when he picked it up. No one ever asked about the border towns, and certainly not someone as odd as the man or elf sitting across from him.

"Splendid!" the man said in a light tone.

Although he was larger than any of the farmers in the area, his skin hung on him in an irregular fashion. Something was off about it, like it had been forced onto him. He reminded Eldritch of an overstuffed sausage.

The man squirmed and placed his arms onto the table around the book, flipping through the pages with an apparent appetite for knowledge. The same Eldritch shared. But this man hunched over it as if devouring a massive feast. His great forearms stretched the ends of his shirt to the point the seams were breaking.

Eldritch held back his laughter at the sight.

"Looks easy enough to get to," the man said. "The name's Grinley, by the way. Sorry, forgot to introduce myself."

"Pleased to meet you." He shook the man's hand. His own felt like a child's in comparison. "Might I ask where you are from?"

"You can ask, but you wouldn't believe it anyway. Let's just say many places." Grinley tapped the side of his nose and winked.

"Keep him longer," the ghastly voice whispered. Eldritch glanced to the back room.

"Before you leave, I have to ask, what are you searching for in Caetheal? Is it for the fae or for their trade goods?"

"So you do know about them, eh?" Grinley slipped his hat back on and tucked his hair into it. "Ever seen one before?"

"I have seen some in illustrations. But I believe they would be brighter than any precious gem."

"That they are, that they are." Grinley leaned back again and the chair let out a small creak. "One like yourself should be wary though." His voice grew darker and he wrung his hands together. "Your stature would be easily plucked for their services. They should be feared more than admired. Their magics are not to be taken lightly or as whimsical tricks."

"What do you know of their magic? These books do not contain much knowledge of it."

"You should join me on my journey. I believe you would thrive in Caetheal."

Eldritch nearly fell against the table at the proposition. He stared into eyes that looked wiser than the rest of the man's appearance portrayed. Grinley appeared trustworthy, but with harvest coming soon and Sayeh. . . He was overcome by the guilt of what he did to her, and there would be no one to watch over the bookshop.

"I suppose that's a bit too much to ask such a lad." Grinley stood up and grabbed Eldritch's arm. "A fae's secrets are likely too wonderful and terrible for any of us to understand anyway."

"If you could stay a couple of days, I could make arrangements to travel with you," Eldritch offered.

"I really must be off now." Grinley nodded sharply and turned toward the door. "Thank you for directing me on my path."

Eldritch witnessed a change in Grinley when he reached for the handle. His hand shrunk to a more manageable size. He covered it with the other while he stepped out onto the street.

Eldritch peeked out the window. Grinley's mouth was moving, but he couldn't make out what he was saying.

Grinley's hands dropped down again to reveal both the same size. With a tilting of his hat, the strange man turned the corner into the alley and was gone.

The sunlight faded in the windows as a dark cloud loomed outside. The door swung open again. Eldritch nearly jumped out of his skin.

"Eldritch?" Sayeh's voice echoed in the shop. "Sorry, I'm so late. Are you in here?"

"Did you see the man who left here a moment ago?" Eldritch said. "He was large and would have been going the other direction."

"I must not have been paying attention." She moved behind the table quickly without making eye contact.

"Are you okay?" Eldritch tried to move closer to see her, but she stepped farther around the table.

"I didn't want to come out." She sighed. "I know people are talking and everything. I didn't want them to see it now."

"What do you mean? What happened? Did your leg get worse?"

"I don't know. I wasn't sure if I should show you. It's strange. I hope you won't see me differently."

"Of course not. I value you more than anything."

41

He stopped. The words came out before he could stop them. He valued her more than any other person, but the thought of choosing her over magical knowledge or power. . . the doubt crept from the dark places in his mind. He shook it off.

"What is it that you want to show me?" he asked and noticed a spark of hope building in Sayeh's eyes. Something he hadn't seen since she fell.

"It will go away in time, won't it?" Sayeh sat in a chair and rolled up her dress. "It needs to finish healing, right?"

Eldritch stepped around the table.

The ashen shell had broken off from her leg. Her knee was free to bend again. However, in its place was a dark scar with twisted lines that ran up her thigh. The entire area was pitted across the skin. It resembled the bark of a tree after it had been scorched in a fire—a severe contrast to the rest of her porcelain skin.

Eldritch realized his hand was over his mouth, and he tried not to gasp.

"Does it hurt?" he managed to ask.

"No. I woke up and it was like this." Her voice quivered. "I tried to scrub the area, but it didn't do anything." Tears formed in her eyes. "I'm so sorry Eldritch, you probably think I'm some sort of monster now."

He couldn't help but stare in amazement. He held out his hand.

"Can, I touch it?"

Sayeh choked on her tears. She gave him an embarrassed smile and moved her leg away. She sobbed again and pulled her dress back down, shaking her head.

"I'm sorry." She sighed. "It feels so strange and unnatural. I can hardly believe it's my leg."

"Well, at least you can do some of the work around here again." Eldritch forced an awkward smile and hoped his attempt at humor would be well received.

Her eyes narrowed and she did not respond.

"I'd been meaning to ask you about something," he continued and cleared his throat. "Do you know if there is a way to get to that lower level? Not through the floor of course."

"Why didn't you build a door or entry when you fixed it if you want to go back down there so badly?" Her tone was bitter and sharp.

"I didn't want any more of the floor beams to break." He stumbled over his words, each one making Sayeh's anger appear more intense. "Are there any other hidden rooms?"

"You know, for a man stuck in books all day, you really don't understand much!" She picked up the book that had the maps spread out to Caetheal. "Can you get these organized or am I going to have to pick up after you all day?"

"I'm the only one in here most of the time." He looked back to the storage room. "Could I dedicate a shelf to the ones I use the most? Maybe that would help keep this place clean. I don't want to put extra strain on your leg."

"I can manage on my own," she said through gritted teeth and clenched her fists. "Your family probably needs you for the harvest time. You best get back to them and stop coming here."

She limped away from the table.

The hair stood up on the back of his neck. Her words fell heavy on his heart. He slowly walked to the door and turned back before he left.

"I'm sorry, Sayeh," he whispered and closed the door behind him.

4

Eldritch tried to focus on helping his parents with the harvest, but he could not stop thinking about what happened to Sayeh. Although it was not quite two weeks, each hour strung out like years since he was last at the bookshop.

He hung his head at his desk and stared at the paper in front of him. An apology letter was what he attempted to write, but a blank page was all that remained in front of him. As much as he tried to stay awake and craft an elegant poem to beg her forgiveness, his eyelids grew heavy and started to close. He rested his head on his arm. The pen in his other hand scribbled something out as he faded into his dreams.

Seeker, do not falter. Secrets have begun to stir.
Seeker, the time is nigh. You know the answer.
Rise with the moon. Set course to fly.
All will be revealed soon if you seek her.

The words blurred in his vision as Eldritch rubbed his eyes open. He did not recognize the handwriting. The letters curled into each other and had the appearance of being stained from the other side of the page. He blinked and held his pen closer. Dried ink was smeared across the tip.

He dropped it and stood, allowing the sunlight to bring him back to his senses. Squinting out the window, the day was nearly over. He must have fallen asleep close to morning and wasted most of the day. The sun would soon be setting.

"Mother, I need to get something in town," he called out, hoping no one would respond. "I will return to help soon."

He strained his ear for any movement in the other rooms. They were likely out in the fields without him. They shouldn't mind if he snuck away for an evening like he used to do.

He grabbed the paper and shoved it under his bedroll. With the air getting cooler as summer came to an end, he needed to bring his cloak with him. He grabbed it and headed out the door.

An apology letter would have been nice to give Sayeh, but for now, he'd have to rely on his wit. His worst trait.

"I wondered when you'd show up again," Sayeh said as Eldritch stepped inside the bookshop.

The entire journey to town, Eldritch had been planning how to apologize to her. Now she looked at him in a way that erased his memory of the speech.

"Sorry, there was work needed at the farm," Eldritch mumbled.

"Seems everyone is busy around here. It's been lonely without you."

"It has?" He stepped in farther and placed a hand on the table, wet from a recent spill, or over cleaning. "How is your leg healing?"

"It's—" She pressed her dress down over the place the wound had been. Eldritch could see a bit of extra cloth on her leg. "I don't know. The damned scar is still there. I'm glad it's cooler out so I can cover it better."

"I'm sorry," Eldritch confessed. "I feel like it is somehow my fault for everything."

"It's not your fault. I should be the one to apologize. You saved my life."

"I wish there was more I could do to help."

"There is something you can do," she said with a flirtatious chuckle. "I have something I've been meaning to show you."

Eldritch hoped the sunburn he'd acquired from working in the fields would hide his flushing cheeks, but knew from Sayeh's smile, it didn't.

"I don't think we should try the storage room." He gave a nervous laugh.

"If you're not ready, that's okay," Sayeh said.

"It's not that." Eldritch sighed. "What did you want to show me?"

"A secret. I'll show you if you agree to come with me."

His feet wouldn't move. He wasn't sure if he was even breathing.

Before he could respond, she grabbed his hands and pulled him from the door.

"What are you doing?" Eldritch managed to say when she slipped behind him.

A familiar clicking sound of the key locking the door made him sweat.

Sayeh kept her grip on him. She was either getting stronger or he was getting weaker. He needed to show her that he had some confidence.

"Okay," Eldritch said grabbing her hand tighter. "I'm ready to go."

"If you will follow me." She bowed down in her corset that had been loosened. Her hair tumbled onto her face. She slipped the strand behind her ear and grinned.

Eldritch's mouth had fallen open when she bent down, and he was likely staring too hard. She had a way of working a magic over him that he could not explain.

Obediently he followed her toward one of the back shelves.

"I found it while sorting these books. I believe they were riddles that have been solved or notes on puzzles from what I could read." She paused. "Thank you again for teaching me. I wouldn't have figured it out without you. I hope once you see it, you will accept my proper thanks."

Sayeh moved one of the larger books away to reveal three small holes in the shelf. A faint ring of worn wood circled around them. She grabbed a nearby book and flipped it on its spine.

The clasp matched the three holes, and with a push, the book turned. She looked back to Eldritch with a wild expression.

"I didn't have time to clean much, but there's surprisingly no spiders or rats, which is odd considering the amount we get in the attic. I'll never go up there again. Likely to become a feast for them up—" She bit her lip and looked back to the shelf. "I'm babbling on. Let me show you. I, well, you'll see."

She pressed the book into its former place. As it sunk into the shelf, a section of the wall beside it swung open. Stairs descended into the darkness.

He couldn't determine if his hands were shaking from excitement or nervousness as Sayeh grabbed them again.

"Sorry, can you go first?" she asked. "The dark scares me a little, and I need to grab a light. I can meet you down there."

Eldritch nodded. Her words sounded miles away. His mind was already climbing down the darkened staircase. Instead of a dread keeping him still, a lure to enter tugged at his soul.

The air gave no scent of decay or rot. A passage to nowhere and yet, everywhere. And perhaps the answers he sought.

Only the light spilling in from the entryway would have to guide him. No windows were available to lend him aid.

Hollows of the Nox

His better judgment told him not to reach along the walls. He imagined grabbing fistfuls of spiders or other creatures that liked to burrow in such forgotten places. But he could not resist.

His fingers stretched out along the wall to steady his descent. Smooth and hard, like coal or marble. The space was sealed tight enough that a breath wouldn't be able to enter. He felt intrusive on the sacred tomb. The first one to cross the threshold in ages.

The bottom of the stairs expanded into a corridor. The world above him faded from existence while he traveled farther. He had to be close to the main chamber.

His left hand dropped into an opening to another room. The smooth surface on his right cornered in as well. The doorway and the walls extended out beyond his reach.

This was the room.

He wanted to remember the layout, but the brief glimpse he had weeks ago did not give him enough information. The light from the opening of the stairs gave him no assistance either. It was an encompassing blackness.

He tried to step into the room, but his foot hit an object. The impact shifted his weight forward as he fell into the abyss before him. The ground seemed to come up at him.

His shoulder ached. All sense of direction was gone. Putting pressure on his arm to sit up caused a spike of pain. He gritted his teeth and shook off his suspicions. Nothing broken.

A soft glow filled the doorway from where he had fallen. The light bobbed slowly down and became brighter as the source approached the open room.

"Eldritch?" Sayeh's voice whispered from the corridor.

"I'm in here." Eldritch coughed and rolled onto his back. "I must have tripped on—"

Sayeh stepped into the room. Her skin glowed in the candlelight, exposed by her low cut robe. She smiled.

"You are beautiful," he stammered trying to think of a better way to describe her, but his mind was dizzy from the fall and the way the silk clung to her body.

Her leg showed the scar as she stepped closer to him.

"Did you fall? Are you hurt?" She placed the candle on a stack of books an arm's length from his head.

He was speechless as she bent toward him. She had changed from the awkward girl he befriended in the bookshop, to a woman he found himself lusting after now. It was almost unbearable.

He turned away and looked at the ceiling. The boards were formed tight together, except one area. Where Sayeh had fallen. The same charred formation that infested her leg scabbed over the wood.

Her hand rubbed his leg.

"I will let you explore these chambers," she said. "But first, you must explore me."

The pain in his side came back, but he paid it no heed as he pushed himself up to her embrace. Her warm skin shivered at his touch. She curled inside his arms and softly kissed his neck.

She moved her lips to his, and his mind floated in celestial bliss. The kiss shattered time and all his insecurities. She was all he needed, all he desired.

She stopped kissing him and coughed.

Eldritch opened his eyes again. Something in the air burned into his nostrils.

"What's that smell?" He noticed one of the books emitting a cloud of gas.

The vapors clouded his vision, but he could see the ceiling glowing and smoking with the same eerie cloud.

A pain shot through his arm from Sayeh's fingernails digging into his skin.

Her scream echoed through the catacomb.

She released Eldritch and he crawled away. He could taste blood mixing with the sulfuric residue in the air.

"Get it off! Get it off me!" Sayeh cried.

She collapsed to the ground scratching at the scar on her leg. It too smoked and cracked with the rest of the room. The light from the candle intensified with a surge of energy. The ceiling turned to a deep red glow like coals in a fire.

"It's this place," Eldritch said grabbing her. "You shouldn't be here."

His shoulder burned with pain from the fall as he lifted her from the ground. He had to get her out. The scar turned a deep red.

Sayeh's tears and sobs stopped between her cries of pain while he carried her up the stairs. He clenched his teeth through the grip of her fingers clawing into his back.

At last, they reached the top. Eldritch laid her down and she collapsed onto her dress from before. She must have thrown it off in haste to slip into the robe.

She cowered in the garments, trying to cover her leg and shaking from the shock.

"Please, let me help you," Eldritch said between breaths. He pulled a cloak from his bag and wrapped it around her.

"I'm fine now," she said in a whisper. "It doesn't hurt anymore. I'm sorry. I wanted to show you how much I care for you."

"I know, Sayeh. I know how much you care for me. You don't need to do anything at all." He couldn't look away from her leg that had swollen around the scar. "I do want to be more than friends."

She smiled at him and stopped rubbing her leg.

"The candle. I think it's still down there. I can't—" She tried to stand but fell back down.

"Stay here. I'll get it."

Eldritch returned to the stairway. A smile crossed his lips as a new desire consumed him and carried him deeper into the chasm. No whispers in his ear were necessary.

The stench from the sulfur hung like a mist low to the ground. Although the candle tried vehemently to light the room, its small flame did little to drive out the embracing darkness.

Scattered shelves of books drew a haphazard circle around the center table. The maps and ancient tomes coiled together in their preserved state. A layer of dust and splinters covered the area where Sayeh had broken through.

Eldritch retrieved the candle to get a closer look. Piles of ash coated the table. It covered all the books, save for one.

Drops of dried blood mixed with the debris around it, but the cover remained unscathed. Its leather skin stretched tightly around the pages, covering whatever mysteries lay inside. It smoldered from the smoke.

Eldritch stepped back in terror. The blood had not missed the book, but it had shaken it off somehow—like a living creature. The book trembled and smoked once more as he stumbled back.

He caught himself on a nearby table, placing his hand onto another strange book. The cover felt similar to wet grass. As he moved his hand away, the illustration twitched from his touch.

This one did not strike him as evil. He brushed the cover again, watching the plants in the artwork sway under his fingers, before opening it.

The crude illustrations of plants looked to be done by an unskilled illuminator, yet the words around each drawing required a master calligrapher. The language was indistinguishable. The shapes and patterns jumbled together, mashed from different dialects like a combination of languages.

He traced his fingers along the drawings and words. The picture looked more alive than not. It began to have depth and volume and reached up from the page.

As Eldritch grabbed onto the illustration, the plant stretched and pulled itself from the paper. He held it closer. A new species. Its roots and leaves were almost familiar but from separate plants. The flowers upon it were altogether strange. He placed it beside the book that had the old crude drawing of the plant on the page again.

Eldritch turned to the other book still smoking and shaking. Like the sensuous lure in Sayeh's eyes, it beckoned him to touch, to take whatever he wanted from it.

No. Something sinister about the way the blood pooled away from it. He was not ready.

He grabbed the small plant and the book that it came from. It would require more study to unlock its mysteries, and he didn't want to leave the chamber empty-handed.

The dark book let out a shrill cry. Eldritch felt the desire for it again. He could grab it too. There was plenty of room for both in the bag he carried.

He inched closer, the desire to read it growing stronger with each step.

There were no words on it. Only the symbol of a tree which seemed to grow into the book itself—like the scar on Sayeh's leg. The roots appeared to hold the pages together inside its locked seal.

The blood around it sizzled. Sayeh's blood. She had to be worried. He left her alone for too long.

His hands reached for the book against his will.

"No!" he yelled.

He thought he heard growling as he struggled against the power driving him closer.

"Let me free!"

A force rammed into his chest, knocking him and the candle over with one last burst from the wick.

He could hear the book boiling in Sayeh's blood. It gave him direction in the darkness, the opposite way to get out.

He crawled through the entry and climbed into the dim light.

"Sayeh, are you there?" Eldritch reached the top of the stairs and found his cloak lying on the ground where she had been. "The candle fell over, and I couldn't find my way out."

No response. The pulsating of his heart and the strange sounds of the dark book echoed in his ear. Maybe he should have grabbed it.

"No one should know what is down there," he said to himself. The power would be too great for a weaker mind, it was almost too great for his. He needed to be stronger.

He pushed on the other side of the shelf to close the secret doorway. It gave a low thud and locked into place. The book that turned the locking mechanism was not there.

"Did Sayeh take it?" he muttered to the empty room.

The trance from the book could have lasted for hours or seconds. There was no distinct way of knowing and the only remaining light coming in was from the moon.

He hated himself for leaving Sayeh, but she had likely gone home. Any chance he had with her that night extinguished with the candle. The thought of the dark book in the chamber made him tremble. He needed time away from the bookshop.

"We will wait, we are always waiting." The familiar whisper came again. This time it crept outside his mind, somewhere in the direction of the hidden door.

Eldritch shook his head and checked to make sure the other book of plants remained in his bag. He would have plenty to study for a while, and his parents would need him for the harvest. The cellar would wait for him to return. When he was ready.

5

"Eldritch, wake up! You'll never believe this son." His dad's voice was followed by banging on the door to his room. "We will have to get an early start to get all of it collected. Meet us at the grove as soon as you are ready."

Eldritch groaned and sat up. The sun had not entered his room yet. Although the mysterious plants from the book created a mixture that helped his body sleep less, it was more precious to him now. His entire meditation would need to be restarted—later.

He pulled his blanket off and stumbled toward the book of plants. Dried leaves and fragments of roots littered the table. He needed to focus on the correct ingredients to make him more alert. When he first discovered the mixture, he consumed it too late in the night and slept for most of the next day.

Of course, the directions gave little aid on when and how much he should use. The language of the book was a jumble of old and new words, more so than the compounds of herbs and plants it produced from its pages.

"Where are you?" He flipped through the pages, trying to keep his eyes open.

He turned to the page with the bright green plant that had clusters of red berries. They needed to be dried and roasted before giving the proper effect. He grabbed a handful and started downstairs.

"Is anyone here?" he called out to the empty house.

His father wasn't joking about leaving right away. His parents had already gone out to the apple trees. There was no time to prepare the berries. Perhaps he could find a way to roast them and make them into a drink. He shook his head.

"One thing at a time," he muttered and jammed the berries into his mouth, spitting the seeds into a container. They could be used later.

The sweet juices made him choke on some of the pits. He took a swig of water and stuffed the extra fruit into his pocket. Their magic would give him more energy while he walked to the grove.

He understood his father's surprise when he arrived at his family's apple grove. The red, green, and yellow fruit glistened in the morning light, nearly twice the size of an average crop. With the drought, his parents had been searching for even a bucketful of edible ones.

"You came quicker than he thought," his mother said meeting him on the path. Her wheelbarrow overflowed with apples. "We may need to use the horse and the larger cart to get all of these in today. Whatever strange smelling concoction you put around these trees really worked."

"I told you they would work," Eldritch said. "But I wouldn't have guessed it would be this much."

"Where did you find the information on that anyway?"

"I've been studying books on how some of the other cities can thrive during droughts," he lied.

No one could know the secrets of the plant book he found. While most of them were for growing and harmless spells, some were more like poisons and could wipe out entire populations.

"Well, we appreciate the help around here." His mother lifted the wheelbarrow up. "I hope you're not just helping us because you are avoiding Sayeh."

Eldritch stared at the ground in silence and kicked a stone along the path.

"Some of the others have been saying she hasn't been right lately. Tell your father I'll get the horse."

Eldritch nodded and looked down the path to the grove. The town rested farther down with Sayeh and the bookshop. He hadn't returned since their last encounter. He couldn't bring himself to check on her after his embarrassment.

The time of the harvest was passing quickly as his days mixed with his nights. He studied as much as he could, yet the magic he used on Sayeh's leg eluded him. The recipes he found in the plant book would help someone heal faster or numb the pain, but there was nothing like the shell that formed around her leg.

"Hey, son." His father waved at him near one of the outside trees whose branches hung low with the heavy fruit. "Can you get the horse for us? Your mother keeps running the wheelbarrow back and forth."

"She's getting it now with the cart." Eldritch grabbed an apple and placed it on top of an overflowing barrel.

"Remarkable isn't it? Not any marks of a pest or rot. Almost like they formed overnight."

"They might have," Eldritch said under his breath. He stepped over a dark root that curved up from the tree. "What is that?"

"Come." His father motioned for him to follow. "I reckon it is where all of the nutrients are coming from for the trees. I've never seen one like it in any of my travels."

"Not that you travel much," Eldritch muttered once his father was out of earshot.

More of the dark roots spiraled around the trees to the center of the grove, the source of the power. A looming aura of strong magic pervaded the air. The sounds of the chirping birds faded from the place.

In the midst of the grove, a lone tree reached up from the ground. It was waist high, but Eldritch sensed it contained more power than he could fathom. He had seen such a tree before—on the cover of another book.

The dark tree seemed to be pulling him closer. The lure of destiny. He needed to get back to the cellar.

"Let's get as much harvested today as we can." Eldritch turned to his father and placed a hand on his shoulder, trying to hide his grimace. "I'm sure it will be good to pick tomorrow as well."

"We will surely have more than enough this season." His father crossed his arms and smiled. "You've been working a lot lately. After today, you should take some time off. Maybe visit that bookshop you're always running off to."

Eldritch looked up to meet his father's gaze. He nodded. His father likely thought he wanted to go see Sayeh, but it didn't matter, whatever got him back to the cellar, and the book. But he couldn't do it during the day, he would have to sneak there under the cover of night.

He had much to plan when he returned to his room. Though the sun had recently descended over the horizon, he needed to start his sleep cycle. To make sure his parents would not notice him, he slipped a special mixture into their drink while they ate that evening.

Their snoring echoed up from the room downstairs. They probably didn't make it past the table.

Sneaking into the town at night could cause suspicion. It was best to remain unseen. He scrounged for his longest cloak to dye. The color had to be dark. Darker than the shadows. One with the shadows.

"*We will help you,*" the voice whispered at him. "*Unlock the words.*"

He thought back to the tales of bandits who would inscribe their garments with symbols allowing them to slip through dark places. Doors of pure shadow. The fabric could be purchased from great enchanters in larger cities.

It was too late to try to purchase one from an enchanter, even if he knew one. He should have followed Grinley. All the books in Raikrune contained stories of the magic, not the spells themselves.

"I do not truly belong here," Eldritch said to himself.

He thought he heard the voice echo his words. The voice that crawled into his mind and unlocked his ability to heal Sayeh. He had used an enchantment, and it ran into the blood-soaked pants from that fateful night, draped over his chair.

He snatched it and threw it in a basin full of his writing ink. If any residual magic remained, it would enhance the spell. His cloak drank up the ink instantly when he dipped it in.

An odd sensation filled his mind, and his voice seemed to be whispering in through the breeze. He pulled the cloak back, completely dry. The enchantment created a fabric blacker than a starless night.

The last glow of the sunset from outside faded away, and clouds blanketed the sky. The darkness would be perfect. No one would see him coming. If not for the mixture of plants to aid him, he too would be lost in the shadows.

All would be revealed from the pages of the book that smoldered in Sayeh's blood and in his mind. He could not ignore its power. He had to see the book again. He had to meet the source behind the voice creeping in the corners of his mind. The voice that gave him the power to heal Sayeh. The voice that, if he listened intently, whispered to him now.

"At the middle of the day, the light is full. In the middle of the night, we are full. Seek us to find us. A worthy man of the book. You understand us. You can bring us here. Free us. We wait for you. When the moon peaks. When the harvest is ripe. Reap the rewards we have for you. Find us as we found you. In time, all comes to clarity. We wait, we watch, we are prepared."

The bookshop seemed to peer back at him, waiting to receive its guest like it knew he was coming. An unknown aura hung around it.

"Is this truly what I want?" he whispered to the old building.

Although the voice was terrifying, it knew about the fae, perhaps it was part of the magic in the forest. The fae had been his desire, his drive for knowledge since he learned of them. Their unearthly ways surpassed those of the elves and humans alike. They spoke to the elements, and the elements listened.

Eldritch pushed on the door, ready to unlock it. It creaked open without the key.

The room sat dark with no candle or smell of a recent flame. He paused, letting his senses adjust to the dank room. The scent of the ancient books filled his nostrils in a euphoric way. The nostalgia of years lost between their pages. Secrets none had seen for decades, centuries.

Even with the aid of his herbal blend, the totality of night made it hard to see anything at all. He would navigate by memory. The wooden floor gave its groans of weight upon it. The oldest boards could be avoided. He remembered those.

Moving like a shadow through the building, he made his way to the back wall. As he came upon the shelf leading to the underground passage, his hand slipped forward. It had been pushed back already.

He gasped.

"Who's in here?" he whispered into the abyss.

Not the slightest breeze or shifting of temperature gave him an indication to what might be lurking in the recesses of the building, only darkness. He stretched his legs into the opening and hunched over, stepping farther into the passageway he dreamed of since discovering it.

The silence was aggressive. His ears wanted to hear the boiling book or the creaking of the ceiling heating and cooling above the chamber. He tried to steady his heartbeat and held his breath to listen, but the complete silence of the room amplified every sound.

He reached into his bag and slid his fingers across the waxy surface of the small candle he brought. He stopped.

Whatever entered before him could still be down there. Maybe it too was blind in the dark and waiting for a glimmer of light to show where to attack.

He trembled and stalked forward.

At last, his outstretched hands found the old wood of the center table. He ran his fingers through the ash and dried blood where the ceiling had collapsed. It hardened into a crust and then, nothing.

The book was gone.

Whoever opened the shelves must have taken it and ran out.

"What now?" he asked the empty room. "Where are you when I am seeking you?"

The voice that once directed him gave not the slightest hint as to where the book could be. In fact, he almost felt it mocking him from beyond the shadows, watching in amusement at his foolishness. He had to be certain it was gone.

He quickly drew his knife and flicked it across a piece of flint. The flash of light from it made him stumble back. The candle's wick ignited and glowed brightly into the room, to his dismay.

The book he once had within his grasp was nowhere to be found.

He pounded his fist on the indentation where the book used to be. There had to be something useful he could use. Something like the other book of plants that could increase his powers.

His gaze fell across some open papers on the shelf beside the table, a map of the area north by the sea.

Although the old diagram was missing some roads, it had markings across the area where the fairy forest lay. As if someone had tried to discover the secret to entry into the fairy realm or maybe even succeeded.

Eldritch traced his fingers over the intersecting lines along the border of the trees. He rolled up the map and stuffed it into a nearby case. Another book flipped open when he pulled the strap out from under it. It too contained spells and unusual patterns of words. In fact, each book he looked through held hidden secrets too powerful for an untrained eye.

He sighed. Too much knowledge.

There was no way to keep them all in his bag let alone memorize them. And he knew the lure of the dark book bent his destiny down a greater path.

"It is a shame to keep these hidden," he said to himself. "Maybe others could find a use for them."

He sorted through the ancient parcels containing charms and spells to find ones small enough to fit in his bag. Some of them were so decrepit, they crumbled in his hand. Their tattered pieces fell onto the ruble of discarded books forming around the areas where he rummaged.

Through the ruffling of pages and the beating of his heart, a strange noise echoed down the stairs. Although faint, he'd heard it before—when he pulled Sayeh out of the broken floor. Her conscious was somehow reaching out for his.

Her cry repeated in his mind. A cry of surprise and terror. He could almost see her in his mind's eye, waiting for him at her home. She needed him.

He emerged from the passage and slid the entrance closed.

The darkness no longer hindered him as he ran outside. It drove him in the direction to Sayeh's home, pushing him faster through the shadows.

6

Eldritch stopped to catch his breath when he reached Sayeh's house. His lungs burned as he looked inside the windows. No light came from within, but strange shadows peaked around the corners of the house from behind. The shapes of trees reached toward him with an evil intensity.

Eldritch's body shook from the adrenaline and the sense of dread coursing through his veins. He hoped to find Sayeh in the small grove behind the home.

There she was, looming over a book in the middle of the violent flickering of a candle ring. Her face twisted with terror and excitement. The same silk robe she wore from their night in the cellar had been shredded into strips like ribbons. Her skin shone through the thin scraps of fabric in the moonlight.

Eldritch moved closer but stopped at the glint of a blade. Sayeh pressed the edge of a knife to her hand. It pierced her skin and cut deep inside the flesh. She clenched her teeth through the apparent pain.

Her cheeks ran with tears, but her hand did not run with blood. She muttered something through her grunts of pain. A scar bubbled open and spewed blood onto a piece of parchment next to the book she read from.

The book. The one missing from before. She stole it.

The dark tree on the cover wrapped around the bloody paper while its roots entered the ground, leaving rings of dead grass wherever they touched.

"He will come, he will obey," Sayeh chanted. "Our love will never fester or bleed."

The scar on her hand smoked until it completely boiled off. Her skin looked new when the white smoke lifted away.

"Sayeh?" Eldritch stammered and stepped into the candlelight. "What is this?"

"You're here?" Her eyes did not meet with his. "Are you really here? Who are you?"

"It's me, Eldritch. What are you doing?"

"The shadows, they have freed me. They have freed us. Our love will not be held back now. See how my leg is free?" She moved the shards of silk to show him the fresh skin. The horrid scar no longer marred her leg. It glistened softly in the candles' glow. "Come, feel it, feel me."

The flames reflected in her eyes as her hair hung wildly around her face like the strips of her once whole robe.

"We can't, not here." Eldritch glance at the large window of her parent's house directly behind them. "Let's go somewhere private."

"There is no one here." She moaned softly.

"Where are they?" Eldritch tried to look into her eyes again, but she kept looking down to the book. "Sayeh, where are your parents?"

"They are no longer with us." Her glare struck Eldritch like the knife that pierced her hand. "I had to be free of the scar. It was the only way. They were holding us back anyway. I knew they didn't want us together." She looked over her shoulder. "They were cruel and deserved it."

Eldritch gasped at the charred remains on the grass. The size of two bodies.

"Sayeh, they were your parents!"

Matthew E. Nordin

"Our love is unhindered. We can be together forever, with my new friends."

Eldritch covered his mouth to keep from heaving. He'd read of dark spells consuming and destroying someone's thoughts, a never-ending thirst for more power and corruption, driving one mad in a wake of bodies.

"She does not understand," the voice returned to Eldritch's mind. *"She hinders what we could be, what you are capable of. Do not listen to her. She lies. She is a killer."*

The flames of the candles twirled in small circles.

"Look at it." She pointed to the paper. "Look what I have made for us, we will live forever now. Together in love."

The spots of blood faded into the background as the paper grew larger. The bottom of the page stretched toward his feet, scorching the ground beneath him. Eldritch tried to flee but was being pulled into a trance.

Words from the spell began to wrap around his mind. It would take over him like he had taken over the other man's mind with the rope. Escaping such a dark spell would take a skilled mage or a more complex pattern of magic.

A phrase deep inside Eldritch came out of his mouth. A spell in an ancient tongue he remembered grabbing in the cellar. He could secure his own will and block it from any spell or caster that tried to invade.

He smiled. He could use this ability to control the force of the dark book. They could not command him or tell him what to do, no one would again. The voices knew nothing of this spell, he hoped.

His mind cleared while the pages finished wrapping around him.

The solid ground became like liquid as he slipped into an engulfing darkness. His mind swam under the surface of the earth and pulled his body along. As one would peel off the blankets from a long rest, he removed the shadows and reformed to the physical realm.

Reaching into his pouch, he grabbed a handful of the powder he used on his parents. It would force anyone to sleep if consumed. It was less than he hoped but enough for him to escape.

Sayeh faced the cocoon of pages that formed around him earlier. It twitched in confusion. She turned as he was almost upon her. Her eyes regained their focus.

"Eldritch, is that you? What happened? I feel as if I was dreaming. When did you get here?"

His hand moved up to her mouth while she spoke, spilling part of the mixture on the ground. Her confused look slumped down into an expressionless state. She closed her eyes and wilted to the ground.

"I'm sorry Sayeh." He wiped his hands on her robe. "I do love you, and I will return for you." He bent down and kissed her forehead. "Someday."

He whispered a prayer for her safety to whatever might be listening. But on that night, the only presence listening waited with an open cover at the center of the candles. Eldritch picked up the dark book and set out for Caetheal—the border city to the fae.

No one recognized Eldritch on the path to Caetheal and hopefully, no one would when he arrived. He used the maps he found to guide him along the old roads. Although they were overgrown, they were less traveled and brought less chance of robberies.

He laughed.

No one would be that foolish to rob him. They would meet a fitting end with the spells he carried.

He looked deep into the small fire he had created for warmth. There was less than a day's journey left to Caetheal. Although he could construct a spell to keep him immune to the cooler night air, he enjoyed the fire.

The flames mimicked his burning thoughts. He could not return to Raikrune. Sayeh was likely accused of murder, and his parents would never understand. He hoped he traveled faster than the news of his disappearance and the victims on Sayeh's farm.

"Those farmers talk," he said to himself. "That's all they do. I need to become someone else. Someone like Grinley."

He smiled at the thought of the elf. Surely he too could create a potion or spell to change his appearance. A simple enough incantation would likely be in the first few chapters of the dark book. Yet, he hadn't opened it. It remained hidden inside the inner linings of his vest.

"I need to steel my mind. Then I can steal the powers."

He fumbled through the other book of herbs, pulling from it the items necessary for the concoction to transform his body. The plants dissolved together in the vial of water produced at the last page and he drank the bitter liquid. It did not burn or turn sour in his stomach. The sharp spices expanded inside of him, changing his throat and tongue. A metamorphosis of his vocal cords.

His hand swelled when he rubbed his throat.

"I hope I measured enough," his voice changed to a deeper pitch.

He did not want it to wear off without warning or stay longer than he planned. Although he told Sayeh he would return, he doubted it would happen. Sayeh would likely wait for him, if she had not run away. Perhaps she followed him.

He ran his hands through his hair that continued to grow longer. For now, he needed to press on. Leave behind his thoughts of Raikrune and focus on the town ahead of him.

The town of Caetheal seemed to float before him in ways he heard about but could never imagine. Architectural wonders were strung together by some sort of invisible wire holding them aloft. Each building he passed was more fanciful than the one before it.

Even in his disguise, the best way of not being seen would be to act like the commoners of the town. But this proved difficult as the people were dressed in different collaborations of cultures more wonderful than he found in his readings. Such whimsical displays only possible through fae disguises and tricks.

"I say, you're dressed for a funeral procession aren't you?" a lady wearing a large brassier of fish scales and a furred dress said. She stepped away and studied him with her gaze.

"Apologies, my lady," Eldritch said and brushed his long hair back. "I am looking for lodging. Where would be a good place to have an extended stay?"

"You'll want to follow this road farther in, turn at the statue toward the cathedral, and follow that road past it until you get to the showroom. You should find what you're looking for there. If you are looking for anything that is. But if not, I'm sure you'll find something there you fancy." The lady laughed and turned to ogle the fresh pastries in the shop behind her.

She looked back one last time at Eldritch. He tried to smile, but his grin felt more sinister than friendly.

"What do I look like?" he muttered to himself.

In the transfusion, he didn't have the ability to see how he had changed. He hoped he resembled a human and slipped the cloak over his head.

He needed to blend in somewhere else.

The alleyways of the city had plenty of shade for him to use his cloak's ability to become one with the dark places. He didn't want to raise any more suspicion, and he was starting to prefer the solitude of the darkness.

He turned off the road into an alley. The shadows melded with his cloak, causing him to slip in and out of sight. If anyone saw him, it would be like a glance out of the corner of their eye. With phantom speed he moved to the cathedral, slipping farther away from the main path.

"Such places as these are not for slinking into," a voice whispered beside him.

Eldritch wheeled around to see another man who stood in the shadows, fading in and out of his vision. His cloak had similar markings on it.

"I am curious," the stranger continued. "Where did you receive your cloak? The craftsmanship is weak at best, but it has powerful enchantments on it."

"It is my own creation." Eldritch proudly stepped out to show his work.

"Interesting. I assumed you had stolen it from one of us."

"And who are you exactly?" Eldritch said more to himself than to the stranger.

The shadows bulged with hoods. More cloaked figures stepped in full view while others peered out from under their shaded covers.

"Travelers like yourself, I assume." The man paced as he spoke. "Forgive me for not introducing myself, but I fear you will not get that luxury. You see, you are in for all sorts of disappointment today." The shadows around Eldritch erupted with more of the hooded men, surrounding him. "It is nothing personal. I admire your craft. We rarely find others who travel from the western ports, but when we do, they often travel in the shadows to carry large amounts of treasures with them. Treasures they try to hide from the petty thieves who lurk about these parts."

Eldritch wanted to run but the way the man studied him, it would end in disaster. He had to have something that could help him escape. His mind went blank.

"So, you're not thieves?" he said, trying to remember a spell, any spell.

"Oh yes, we are thieves—just not petty ones." The man's laughter caused those around him to jeer as well. "If you would be kind enough to remove any valuables you may be carrying, we assure you your passage from here will be safe. If you will not be so kind, neither will we."

The other thieves pulled daggers and other weapons out of the shadows that concealed their forms.

Eldritch glared as he slipped his hand into his pouch. He had a powerful enough spell to stop all of them. . . somewhere.

"Let's keep your hands in front of you so we can see them." The stranger rested his hand on the sword dangling from his belt. "We wouldn't want you doing anything foolish."

He nodded to the shadows beside Eldritch. Two larger men stepped out. Their stature in their dark cloaks made them look like ancient guardians.

"I was simply trying to give you what I have." Eldritch stooped down to look in his bag. "Trust me, it's nothing of interest."

"We are good in our trade. I'm sure we can use anything you have. The cloak, for starters."

Eldritch had to distract the two men towering over him. He slipped off his cloak and gave it to the men with his left hand. His right hand grasped whatever concoction it could find. With precision, he loosened a tiny bottle from his bag and drew back to flick it at the leader of the thieves.

It wouldn't move.

Someone grabbed his hand from the shadows.

"Why would you be so unkind to do something like that?" A duplicate of the leader squeezed his hand. The man he originally targeted for the attack dissipated into a mist with the shadows. "And what do we have here?" He pried the small container from Eldritch's grip.

"You can open it and find out," Eldritch shot back.

The two men who had taken his cloak restrained his arms.

"Perhaps later. Let's see what else you have for us."

The pain made Eldritch almost collapse as the men stretched out his arms. The leader smiled and cut the bags and pouches off Eldritch's garments. All he had belonged to them now.

Beads of sweat stung his eyes. He couldn't focus. If he would've stayed on the street and not worried about his appearance, he wouldn't be in this position. A reckless mistake.

"What is this?" The leader stepped back and opened the bag of spells and maps. He rifled through them and grinned. "I am not sure who you stole these from, but they are rare indeed. Unfortunately, you probably do not know their price. We will relieve you of that burden."

The man stared at Eldritch and walked towards him.

"What other tricks are you hiding in your sleeve?"

He ran his hand along Eldritch's vest, the place where he hid the dark book.

"Ah," he exclaimed as he pulled it free. "Now this is something I have not seen before. Where in all the realms did you acquire this book? Such a wonderful design and quality. It appears ancient, yet new."

Eldritch opened his mouth to speak, but nothing came out.

The leader quickly dropped the dark book to the ground and stepped back. He wiped his hands furiously on his coat. The smell of sulfur filled the alley.

"My hands!" He gasped, no longer with that boastful grin, but with a look of terror. "This is dark fae magic! Leave now!"

As swift and silent as they appeared, the hooded thieves sunk back into the shadows and were gone. The leader ducked into the area where he first appeared, still rubbing his hands on his cloak. He eyed the book one last time before giving Eldritch another fearful stare.

"I don't know what you found, but some things are best left unfound." He narrowed his eyes. "You would do well to distance yourself from it as well."

The man vanished, and Eldritch stood alone. His cloak and other items stripped from him.

The single remaining item he possessed lay in the alley. Smoke rose playfully from it in a ghostly manner. The book had a will and a voice that whispered into Eldritch's mind. Perhaps it had a benevolent reason which saved Eldritch from the thieves.

Yet the leader's warning stuck with him. What was the dark fae magic?

7

The double-story tavern looked to be something from Raikrune, yet twice the average size. A large porch wrapped around the edges of the building, full of tables and chairs haphazardly pushed to the wall.

The dust shook on them as Eldritch stepped up to the double door entrance.

The place revealed its exotic allure when he walked in. Various tapestries hung on the walls, depicting scenes from the farthest reaches of the world. Eldritch recognized many from illustrations in the books he studied. Their bright colors and intricate weaves caused him to stare in admiration.

He would have observed them longer if not for the commotion at the other end of the tavern. In front of a few rows of chairs stood a large man upon a platform stage.

"And now," the man said to the small audience who sat on the edge of their seats. "Witness as I make this simple rope my pet."

A few members of the crowd clapped. Eldritch found an empty table and decided to watch the entertainment. It would be amusing to see what a fellow conjurer could do. He needed a laugh.

The older man made the rope twist up and down his arm. He tossed it to the ground, and it stood up on end like a snake, coiling near his legs.

Eldritch held back his urge to scoff at the simple charms. Such deceptions he had mastered from his studies in the bookshop— mere illusions and sleight of hand tricks meant to mimic true magic. True magic could change the natural to whatever one willed. If their will was superior.

"Slide into my words," Eldritch whispered. "Twist and coil yourself. Your actions are my thoughts."

Something deep within him reached out to control the rope from the strands of clear wire the illusionist used. It slithered to the edge of the stage and formed a coil as it had earlier.

The man on stage gave the rope a confused look and bent down to retrieve it. The end rose from the center. It waved in the air, waiting for Eldritch's command.

"Once tormented, now torment," Eldritch whispered.

At once the rope struck the man as a snake. His frightened and surprised scream caused the audience to break into laughter. The man gave a concerned smile and bowed. As he did, the rope leaped and coiled around his arm.

"Ah! Get it off, get it off!" he cried, flailing his arm around.

The audience erupted again. Eldritch released his enchantment, and the rope fell to the ground.

"Uh, thank you, ladies and gentlemen." The man bowed again and shoved the rope back into his bag.

Eldritch joined the applause while the man stumbled back to the curtain. Some of the crowd threw coins and other precious items onto the stage. Another man stepped out from behind the stage to collect the items in a jar.

"That was some trick, eh?" a familiar voice said behind Eldritch. "The name's Grinley, but I deduce we have met before."

The man pulled over a chair and graciously joined Eldritch's table. Though his voice remained the same, his shape had changed to a leaner size—almost feminine. His hair also changed from the tattered gray to a mossy green.

"I see I am not the only one who has dabbled in disguise spells." He nudged Eldritch in the arm. "By the way, your nose has fallen off."

Eldritch gasped and reached up to his face. He felt around his nose and pulled on it slightly. It was firmly attached between his eyes.

"No, it hasn't."

Grinley laughed and slapped Eldritch on the back. "You don't know how long I've waited to do that to someone. You're the young lad from Raikrune aren't you? Tell me, what brings you up here?"

"I was inspired by your traveling spirit," Eldritch said. "I've often read about this place, and the owner of the bookshop—" He stopped at the thought of Sayeh. He was the only one who knew what happened that night. She could take care of herself. Once he learned more about the book and the dark fae magic, he could return for her. "She didn't need my help anymore."

"Well then, I suppose I'll see more of you. I must say though, I'm sure you have a name other than lad. What did they call you back home?"

"I'm Eldritch."

He coughed. He shouldn't have given his real name. The people from Raikrune liked to spread rumors, and he ran away from home. His parents would start to worry, especially with Sayeh's family gone. Returning to that town would be worse than the encounter with the shadow robbers.

"I had a run in with some thieves on my arrival here," he continued. "They took most of my possessions and all of my gold. Do you know of any place I could stay?"

"Ah, Eldritch. This is the place you want to be." Grinley rubbed his hands together. "They have room here to spare, and gold or jewels are no good to them. You are in Caetheal, the realm of the fairy traders. Gold can be conjured up from shells and stones. What they really want is something I believe you have acquired. I noticed your hidden talents with magic. No doubt from all the time you spent in those books."

"I do, but how does that help me stay here?"

"That's the price, you see. You put on a good show, and the place gets the tips. The more lucrative the show, the better the room. We may need to work on your showmanship, but I know someone who could help with that."

"Do you?" Eldritch grinned. "Well, if he is anything like you, I would like to meet him. Your kindness is refreshing in this odd town."

"You haven't seen half of the oddities this town hides. But that's something I'm good at introducing to newcomers. Don't worry, I won't tell too many people where you're really from."

Grinley nudged Eldritch again and headed for the bar. He slipped behind it and stood next to the barkeeper. Although the barkeeper did not turn to face Eldritch, he could see his head bobbing slowly as he and Grinley whispered to each other.

Come to think of it, Eldritch didn't recall seeing the bartender turn around at all. He kept his face hidden in the task of mixing drinks and cleaning glasses. Even to hand them out, he never turned his head to face his customers. Such focus on his work was admirable and a bit unsettling.

Grinley returned to the table and sat with a pleased sigh.

"Well, lad," he said. "You've got one free night, but you better earn it tomorrow."

A man in the audience turned to them, tugging at his wife's sleeve. He must have heard Grinley mention him being in the upcoming performance. Eldritch's smile turned into a nervous laugh as the wife glared at him. One of the other ladies in the crowd leaned over to point him out to her friend. When she turned, the fish-skinned brassier ruffled against the fur she wore. Her hair had been wrapped in shells for the show.

"What have I agreed to?" he muttered to himself.

"Ah good, you're awake," Grinley said barging into Eldritch's room.

He had not been awake until the pounding on his door. Grinley's shouts to enter broke him free from his slumber. With the book of herbs removed from him, he had no way to create the recipes needed to regain his strength through meditation.

"You missed the lunch rush already. I figured you were tired from the travel, but no one should be this tired. Let's get you ready for the evening show." Grinley tossed a bag of coins on the ground and slipped back into the hallway.

Eldritch forced his body up. His muscles ached from the long journey and rest his body lacked. If only the thieves left him one bag of energy seeds. Those bandits needed to be found. He could force them to give his belongings back if he ambushed them. Such a feat would require powerful spells, likely hidden in the book of the dark fae.

He stared at the strange cover of the book he feared to read. The soft leather invited him to open it. He ran his fingers across it and let his hand rest on the spine. An eerie warmth emulated back.

Tucking the book into its place under his vest, he set out to face whatever waited for him downstairs.

A few people hung around the tavern, digging through the remains of their lunch. One man looked to have fallen in a drunken stupor at the edge of the bar. No one else seemed to notice him.

"Eldritch, over here," Grinley said waving him over to his table. "I see you have met Ben already."

Grinley pointed back to the bar. The man passed out at the bar was gone. Eldritch turned back to Grinley and opened his mouth to speak. Nothing came out. The drunk sat beside Grinley with a sober smile.

"Ben doesn't talk much." Grinley leaned over the table and whispered. "When he does, most of us can't make sense of it. But he knows how to dazzle a crowd." He sat back and slapped his hand on Ben's shoulder. "We need to improve this lad's showmanship. Show him something, Benny."

Ben closed his eyes and chanted in an indistinguishable language. He moved his hands in a blur of speed. Within the motion, a light formed. It erupted from inside as he flicked his hands in the air. Fire twisted down his arms and ended around his shoulders, giving one bright flash before extinguishing.

Ben mumbled to them in what sounded like an explanation. Although louder and slower, it made no sense.

"I think Ben said you can do it all the way down your body." Grinley pulled his hair back, revealing the elongated ears of an elf. "If we combine a few of his light stunts with some of the real stuff you know, the rest of the show will be easy."

"If you say so." Eldritch raised an eyebrow at Grinley. He wanted to ask him more about being an elf, but Ben seemed equally as impressive. And he needed to perform well if he had any chance of staying in Caetheal long enough to learn about the fae. "So do you help with the rest of the show?"

"Indeed I do. None of those tricks will be anything if you don't know how to talk to your crowd. That is an easy thing to teach. The hardest part is having the will to stay on stage with all the eyes on you. Not everyone can pull it off. I know of one that can't." Grinley jabbed his thumb toward Ben. "Not to worry though. I'm sure the audience will love you. It would even work for you to stand on the stage with that fair complexion you used to have. Speaking of, we need to fix that transformation spell. You look like a horse ran over you."

"Is it really that bad?" Eldritch ran his hands over his face. "I haven't been able to see myself."

"Ben, do the thing to show him." Grinley waved his hands in a circular pattern around his chest.

Ben nodded and made similar movements. A ring of energy formed a reflective surface suspended in the air. Ben continued to move one hand above in small circles while his other kept the mirror hovering a finger-length above the palm.

"See it now?" Grinley laughed.

Eldritch leaned in to see what his improvised concoction had done to his face. His skin had lines in strange places, proportional to a human's but with slumps sagging low on his cheeks.

"Looks like I need to work on this." Eldritch tried to pull his skin back.

"Not to worry, lad." Grinley dug around in his bag until he withdrew a vial of dark syrup. "Try this. It will taste like a troll's blood, but it will bring your skin back to how it should be. Careful with it. It's not the easiest to make, and you're lucky I had some on me."

Eldritch held his nose and slurped down the mixture. It tasted like a bottle of dried blood with rats floating in it. His gag reflex made him almost lose it all, but he held it back with a hand to his lips.

"Thank you," Eldritch said with a raspy voice.

His body convulsed in focused spasms. Each section of his body shook while it formed back to its original shape. His throat stretched and burned from his vocal cords reforming.

"Back to your old self again." Grinley slapped his hands together. "Now, we need to talk about the audience. Unless you're a regular here, you're going to be coming at them cold. You'll have to warm them up a bit. I like to think casting small charms on the audience helps. But you don't want to hurt them or put them in any real danger. That'll scare them off. Use some cheap conjuration or illusion, then you can throw in some of Ben's tricks."

Ben snapped his fingers. Smoke rose from them and covered his face. When he emerged through the vapors, his eyes shone like fire. His cheeks cracked and smoldered like embers. In a terrifying display, he opened his mouth and yelled. Sparks and molten lava flew from his mouth toward Eldritch.

Eldritch lurched back, and the effect vanished before scorching his face.

"That's a good one," Grinley said. "You don't do that one as often as you used to."

Ben muttered again, and Eldritch took a quick drink. He was glad he hadn't screamed in front of the others, but his face probably gave away his fear. He forced a smile and caught the end of what Ben said. It wasn't an unknown language.

"I try, but you listen none to me."

The language was similar to the mixture of words written in the herbal book. The simple tricks Ben showed them were petty spells compared to what his actual knowledge of conjuration could be. Eldritch tried to recall what Ben had babbled on about earlier.

"That is similar to what you'll be able to do," Grinley said. "Some of them require the use of hand movements and some you'll have to mimic whatever sounds he's making. Good luck with those. It's nothing like anything I have heard. And trust me, I have heard the tongues of a thousand people. Best to smile and nod." He moved in closer to Eldritch. "I don't think he knows half of what we say to him either. Not sure he speaks the common tongue. Ah well, he knows his spells."

"I will try to use what he teaches me for the show tonight," Eldritch said. "I did enjoy reading about the theater and plays when I was younger."

"Aye, you'll find all you've read about and more while here. By the way, I forgot to mention that you should drink a lot of water when you take that elixir. It'll dry you right up."

"This ale is probably not the best for it then?" Eldritch eyed the liquid in the cup he drank from.

"Don't you worry about water. Ben, give the man a drink."

Ben mumbled the phrases again. This time, Eldritch focused on the patterns of words.

"Form the circles, draw the spheres. Water in air and air in all. Cause this air to fall." His fingers fluttered around and pointed above Eldritch's head.

The air grew heavier and a mist formed in front of Eldritch's face. It soon grew large droplets of water that landed on his hair. A stream trickled in front of him. He tried to cup it in his hand but most spilled across and into his lips.

Ben opened his eyes wider. He twisted his fingers together with the shape of a bowl. The phrase he muttered sounded similar to the one that brought the water.

Dust particles swirled together, forming a cup he handed to Eldritch.

"He must like you, lad." Grinley laughed.

Eldritch quelled his thirst from the water falling from an invisible source. He stood and offered the cup back.

Ben waved his hands and blew at the vessel. It dissolved back into dust.

"Air is never empty, always full. Waiting to be formed as clay." Ben muttered.

Eldritch nodded to him in agreement.

Ben shook his head and narrowed his eyes. He looked at Grinley who continued to laugh at the mess on the ground. Eldritch wondered if anyone acknowledged the strange conjurer in such a way.

Ben bent under the table and clapped his hands. The water melded together and returned to the air as Eldritch joined in the laughter, more out of relief.

He would need time to adjust to life in Caetheal and to study the book of the dark fae, whatever it was. With Ben and Grinley on his side, he would not need to worry about the locals bothering him. And if he performed well enough during the shows, they would leave him alone to study too.

He would strengthen his will to unlock the book's secrets. He stopped. He'd been rubbing his vest where it rested. Its shape formed an impression into his skin, like a close friend.

8

"Fire is lighter than air." With those words, the flames intensified under Eldritch.

Although the smoke burned his eyes, the fire didn't produce any heat. His arms floated up before the levitation spell made the rest of his body weightless. More orbs of fire lighted above his head.

"Is that man part fae?" a child questioned loudly in the crowd.

A few members of the audience chuckled.

Unfortunately, it wasn't actual levitation, more of a lingering jump. Eldritch's spells were like smoke and mirrors to the real magic beyond the tree line of the fairy forest. He wouldn't need a spell to fly if he were part fae.

"The fire consumes all impurities." Eldritch descended into the flames below as the orbs grew larger, twisting into his hair. "Until ash remains."

The spell spun around in a flurry of light and smoke. He remained inside the chaotic swirl longer than he would have done on his own. Grinley told him not to rush, but any concept of timing vanished as soon as he stepped on stage. He took a deep breath to calm his nerves. Almost over.

"Save for the immortals." He let out his best theatrical laugh and commanded the flames to die out.

The audience applauded when he bowed at the edge of the stage. Not quite the standing ovation he'd hoped for, but it pleased him. He sensed their longing for more. The ability to do so waited for him, tucked within his vest pocket.

"Great show, lad," Grinley said slapping Eldritch on the back as he joined him backstage. "The crowd may have looked small, but I can tell they were impressed. Good on you. Make the show your own for tomorrow night." He stared intently at Eldritch. "Be careful not to do anything too intense. I assume you know more than you let on."

"I owe most of the show to Ben," Eldritch said. "They liked his fire tricks the most."

Grinley shrugged and led him to one of the tables in the back corner, behind the curtain. A few of the other entertainers sat at a table and had partially consumed drinks in front of them. Grinley mentioned something about a performers' resting area.

"I've been doing this for too long," one of them commented. "It will be good to have new blood in here. Should help all of us."

"You should leave while you still can," another jeered.

"I really do have things to attend to," Eldritch said hurriedly. "I must study and prepare."

Grinley nodded and sat down to speak with the others.

Eldritch rushed upstairs. He had prepared enough to study the dark book. It waited for him in the recesses of his mind. Always lurking within his desires. With the knowledge he'd learned from Ben and the superficial illusions he'd witnessed from the other performers, he was certain he could control its power.

The tree on the cover squirmed under his fingers as he tried to open the dark book. Sayeh must have learned some trick to unlock it. He wondered if she had a choice to open it. It didn't seem possible for her to do without any study.

The book truly had a will and a purpose of its own, but it didn't matter. His purpose was greater. His will was stronger.

"You brought me here, you wanted me to find you," he said to it. "Open and reveal yourself. I am Eldritch, and I command this."

"You speak as one with more understanding of us than you know," the voice echoed around the room. *"We are close, so close now. It is almost time. You can find us in here, but that is not where we enter. We are trapped beneath these pages, in this contraption of skin and ink. Release us, and you will be rewarded. Fail, and someone else will become more powerful than you. They will be given the abilities and secrets we have hidden beyond time."*

"Unlock yourself. Show me."

The book's cover peeled away from the edges. The tree on the front held it closed by its roots. Eldritch grabbed the book and ripped it open the rest of the way. The roots retreated from the pages, shrinking back from the force.

Eldritch's eyes widened at the wisdom exposed to him.

It was impossible to read. The words were unlike the ones in the herbal book. No patterns or repeated phrases. Each word contained an entire story behind the characters. Like looking at the tip of an island in the water, the larger portion of knowledge floated beneath the words, or it floated alone with the illusion of more behind it.

The longer Eldritch stared at the book, the deeper beyond its surface he submerged. The text was not words written in different languages, it was every language contained in single words. Every story or dream locked away in the pages of this book.

He scanned the book and found a page that had been recently torn. The page contained the spells Sayeh had used in an attempt to transform Eldritch's will to her desire, to follow her without question—words of lost love. Lovers who longed for their mate and witnessed it taken away by choice or by death. Each shattered desire and lost hope was locked behind these words. They could be released to live again in another world.

The desires of the reader determined the magic, unlocking the true ability of words. The power to control and change a person's will. With the book's strength, Eldritch could decide the fate of all inside the tavern.

"Such power, how would one know when to stop?" he questioned aloud and trembled. His own will could be turned against him if he did not have enough focus.

The book changed as he continued to read. It was alive, resisting his will over it. In time he would be able to overpower it and use the lost hopes and dreams of others to fulfill his own.

"You understand nothing of our true power," the voice taunted from inside the book. *"You will. Be patient as we are patient. Seek the fae. The beginning is where you will find our prison."*

Eldritch could not control the book any longer. The words swirled into a void on the page too fast for him to read. The cover tree's roots grew through the ink holes. They twisted together at the center spine and pulled the book shut.

Eldritch sighed and rubbed his temples. Controlling his own mind needed to come before controlling the mind of the book. His vision blurred from the new knowledge, and he had already used too much magic during the show. It drained him.

"Tomorrow," he promised as he climbed into bed. "I will find that hidden entrance."

He needed to get his herbal book back. The exhaustion took its toll on him without it. It eventually took over the anger continuing to build against the thieves who stole his other spells. They would pay, once he was well rested.

To Eldritch's surprise, no one else wandered the streets of Caetheal in the early morning. A few of the shop owners bustled about their businesses, but they paid him no heed. He almost wished they would. At least to give him some directions as he was traveling by memory.

Without any maps on what route would be best, he had to stick to the main road, the worn path designed for humans with carts and horses to bring their goods to the city.

"Find the path, get to the forest," he repeated to himself.

It was somewhere west of town, but he wondered if the fae used the trade routes. It wouldn't be too much of a stretch to assume they simply appeared in the stores they needed to be in.

The path stopped abruptly at the edge of a large field. Beyond the area, the trees of the fairy forest stretched in either direction and rose like mountains to the sky. A haze above them hid their actual height.

"There must be a path of entry," he said to the empty field. "Perhaps farther south. Or maybe north near the water. Do fairies like water? Where would a fae leave their forest, if they left at all?"

He adjusted his coat and stepped into the field.

Sharp vines and thorns sprung up harshly from his footfall. The farther from the path he walked, the larger the barbs became.

A scattering of plants popped up from the ground. From his studies with herbs, these were not pleasant ones. With the right recipe, he could be immune to their paralyzing nectar, a recipe he no longer possessed.

No gritting of teeth or ignoring of pain could get him through such a defense at this time. Wherever the entrance was, he couldn't examine it now. The grip of the thorns in his sandals loosened as he stepped back onto the path.

The air smelled of jasmine mixed with vanilla. An aroma he had not smelled since. . . Sayeh.

He turned to the fairy forest again, barely catching the movement of something beyond the field, near the base of the trees. It looked impossible to move between the trunks. They almost grew together in one large form.

The figure appeared again, a familiar shape, but too far away to determine. Eldritch needed to get closer. He took a few steps back into the field.

A wild thorn jammed into his leg, forcing him to retreat again. Blood ran down his ankle. Limping back to the path, he sat down and put pressure on the punctured skin.

"Sayeh?" Eldritch called. "If that's you, I know you're here. You don't need to be afraid."

He stared at the forest, waiting for the figure to return. Nothing. He rubbed his eyes and stood up.

"Whoever is there, I will have you know that I will not be swayed easily by whatever ill you have for me. Come closer, and I shall prove it to you."

He waited. There was no sound except a few birds overhead and his heavy breathing from the pain in his foot.

It couldn't have been Sayeh. There was no possible way she could find him. He never told her how to reach Caetheal or the border lands. Although they did speak about the fae during most of his visits. Yet even with his extensive study, he could never distinguish truth from fancy. Such was the fae magic.

"The field of eternal sleep." He shook off the pain and turned back to the city. "Did she find a way past it?"

Sayeh had somehow unlocked the dark fae book and found the hidden passage under the shop, so understanding his favorite poem he liked to quote to her was possible.

But if it was Sayeh, she would have rushed out to greet him. Unless she hadn't forgiven him. He hung his head and traveled back to Caetheal. The words of the poem echoed down the path in the haunting voice:

Matthew E. Nordin

The fae see you, but you will never see,
Dancing between worlds of reality.
If you linger too close, you will weep,
Falling into the field of eternal sleep.
Let them sing until your heart is free.

9

A small group of locals gathered around the stone well in the center of town when Eldritch returned. Most guffawed over their latest hair accessories and held their hands aloft, letting their rings sparkle in the morning light. Eldritch looked down at his mundane appearance. He did not have anything like their fancier clothes, but he could at least try to fit in a little more. He pulled out the small bag of coins he collected after the show. With any luck, some shops still traded with them, unlike the tavern.

He spotted one of the many tailor's shops. A familiar voice boomed above the crowds before he had a chance to wander in.

"This here, friends, is something exceptionally rare," Grinley said, gathering the people around him and Ben. "Not only is it a useful bottle for containing liquids, it is also a bottle containing a mighty ship for sailing."

The audience around him chuckled. Eldritch moved in closer, eager for a chance to speak with Grinley whenever his stunt completed.

"Ah, you don't believe me. That's all right. Many can't see the ship because it is magic and is only revealed to those with the true sight."

More people snickered while he flipped the bottle into the air.

"I happen to know this, because my friend, Ben, professes it to be true." He cupped his hand over his mouth in a pretend whisper. "I've never been able to see it myself. He might be crazy."

Ben spun his hands around and put them on his eyes. "Just smarter than you is all," he muttered in his strange language.

"See, what did I tell you?" Grinley took a slow swing at Ben with the bottle.

Ben ducked out of the way and stuck his tongue out. He toppled forward a little too easily as Grinley tapped the back of his knee with his foot. Ben held up a fist to react but turned back to the crowd with a mock look of surprise and smiled.

"As I was saying, my friend here can see this great ship inside the bottle but I can not. It would take a true believer who can see beyond the physical to be able to do so. Of course, I think he's bluffing and gave me an empty bottle."

As Grinley spoke, Ben told a strange tale in his unique language. It was something about a ship which sailed the smallest seas, carrying its passengers into tiny harbors. His spell sounded more of a story than a ritualistic chant.

"I'm afraid no one has the sight," Grinley continued. "I might as well put a cork in this and see who would want a simple bottle."

The crowd gasped as smoke formed into a storm inside the bottle. The tiny flashes of lightning swirled into the shape of sails. Soon the entire container was filled with a great ship that fit perfectly inside the once empty bottle.

"I don't know though." Grinley peered into it and turned to Ben. "It is my last drinking vessel, and I'd hate to have to buy another one because of this magical sight you claim to have. There's no real magic in the world. I keep telling you."

"There is magic," a young boy in the crowd exclaimed, pointing at the bottle. "Don't you see it, daddy?"

The child's father laughed and nodded in agreement.

"What?" Grinley put the bottle up to his eyes and squinted, overplaying his act of confusion. "I still don't see anything. Are you sure there is something in there?" He held the bottle out so the audience could get a closer look, and cause a distraction.

Ben stepped back from the others. He muttered again—too softly for Eldritch to hear. His entire form shifted. Instead of the strange man with a scraggly beard, his body slimmed to a feminine shape. His clothes turned into a vibrant purple dress, and his hair grew into long curls.

A few who saw him change laughed and pointed. The new Ben stepped forward to grab the bottle. He batted his eyes at Grinley.

"Oh, excuse me miss, when did you get here?" Grinley said.

Ben giggled and winked at the crowd.

"Oh, well, I suppose you can have the bottle, but be careful with it. It is my last one, and my friend said it was special. Where did he go? Ben? Benny?" Grinley turned to the audience behind him.

Ben held a finger to his lips and giggled again. He lowered the bottle to the boy who exclaimed it was magical. The rest of the crowd clapped when he handed it to the eager child. Eldritch found himself laughing along as Ben twirled his dress and swayed his hips.

"What are you doing?" Grinley said turning back around. "Where did my bottle go?"

Ben held up his hands and shrugged.

"Well if you don't know, I suppose that's all right." Grinley removed his hat and acted shy. "You wouldn't happen to be busy tonight would you?"

Ben took the hat and pulled it over Grinley's eyes. He fluttered his eyelashes at the audience.

One of the ladies laughed louder than the others around her. Ben grabbed her arm and pulled her next to him. He twirled his fingers over her head, transforming her hair to match the color and curls of his, and led the woman over to Grinley.

The crowd cheered as Ben took an elaborate bow. His womanish disguise fell off of him.

Grinley lifted his hat back up and took the audience member's hand, kissing her lightly on the wrist.

"Anytime you feel like that drink, stop by the tavern. We'll be there." He winked at her, and she slipped back to her friends, continuing to blush and smile flirtatiously at Grinley. "Well friends, we must depart. If you enjoyed our performance, we take any trade-able wares or empty bottles. Stop by for more entertainment and delight at the tavern." Grinley put an arm around Ben's shoulders, and they bowed in unison.

The crowd pushed around Eldritch, dropping small items into the large basket in front of them. Quite the amount for a little show. Eldritch took a mental note. The key indeed lied in the way they interacted with the crowd at the beginning.

"There he is," Grinley said, pointing at Eldritch. "We wondered when you'd see us on the road."

"It was an entertaining show," Eldritch said. "You two make quite the pair."

"The masses must be appeased," Ben said in his mumbled language.

"Indeed," Eldritch replied.

Ben looked at Grinley and then back to Eldritch. He fumbled with the corners of his vest.

"Is it true you understand the words of this conjurer?" Ben asked intently.

Eldritch nodded slowly and turned to Grinley. "I wanted to find you—"

"Well, I must be off." Grinley interrupted. "Ben can show you some more tricks if you like."

"Do you have a moment?" Eldritch asked as Grinley began to leave. "I need to ask you. The girl from the bookshop in Raikrune, Sayeh. Have you seen her wandering here in Caetheal?"

Grinley didn't stop or acknowledge that he heard him.

Eldritch glanced at Ben. It was unlikely he would know anything about Sayeh or Raikrune unless Grinley told him.

"She who wanders in your mind does not wander here," Ben said.

"What did he say about her?" Eldritch stepped closer to whisper. "I understand your language. Please, tell me."

Ben nodded to all the people meandering around them. He motioned for Eldritch to follow.

"Sayeh, as she is called, has been mentioned in passing but she is a distraction from your teachings," Ben said once they were farther from the crowd. "You must focus your mind on what is before you. Leave what is past to your memories. Do not try bringing such things with you. Especially through magic. Dark forces corrode the memory and your mind."

"I cannot forget her completely. I promised to return for her once I am strong enough to take her from that place. Unfortunately, most of what I had learned was stolen when I arrived." Eldritch sighed. "You don't know a way of restoring something that was lost to its owner do you?"

"That which was learned always remains with you. Hidden in the secret rooms of your mind. Once unlocked, all becomes clear. Paths are found when returning to the source."

Ben's words sounded familiar. Like the voice that called to Eldritch from the dark book.

He squinted at Ben's face, checking to see any hints of the fairy or elven races. A simple human face like his own stared back with a puzzled expression. Nothing extraordinary except his speech.

"There are many things I know, and few who try to understand," Ben continued. "I do not know where they all come from, only that they are and can be."

"Teach me, I want to learn." Eldritch stepped closer to Ben, eager to take in whatever knowledge he possessed.

"All flows around, all is here, all will obey when your mind is clear." Ben tapped Eldritch's forehead. "Clear yourself of her thoughts."

Ben stepped back and muttered the phrase which engulfed his body in fire. He appeared like an ember, glowing brightly and spewing out flames.

Eldritch tried to repeat the spell. The flames flicked out wildly without control. It surprised him how Ben had such precision with them.

"How did you do it with such restraint and focus?" Eldritch had to know after both of their spells fizzled away.

"Breathe." Ben motioned in and out with his hands from his nose. "All is in your breath. You do not breathe right. The magic must flow as steady as the stream inside of you. Let the energy flow into you and out from you. You become part of the spell, in harmony with the elements. It will bend as you desire. Breathe first and control throughout."

Eldritch focused deeper into the spell and on his breathing. His eyes fogged over like panes of glass. His mind looked out from beyond them, reaching into the atmosphere and borrowing the energy he needed for the spell. He would return what he took from the elements when he finished.

Although not as refined as Ben's, the flames stayed tight to his body. A sense of wonder filled his chest. True power. Yet he did not feel any heat coming from the fire so there was no telling if it could harm anything.

He let the flames fall on a nearby plant. They licked around the green leaves, leaving no mark. An illusion.

The flames flashed around Eldritch as he gritted his teeth. He needed more of the energy in the air. This time he wouldn't promise to return it. It belonged to him.

"You must not let the magic cause destruction." Ben stepped between him and the plant. "It destroys you here." He tapped the temple on his head. "Do not test me on this, trust me."

Eldritch clenched his fist and returned the flames to the place they had been formed. He stared into Ben's worried eyes. That must be how Ben's speech became like gibberish to others. He probably dabbled in more destructive conjuring before meeting Grinley. Those dark spells must remain in the hidden rooms of his mind.

If Eldritch could somehow see into Ben's mind, he could unlock the power holding the elements together, becoming unstoppable. He had read of spells allowing casters to step into the minds of others for information and to control another's will. But those stories ended in madness, more so than Ben's poor soul.

"Can you teach me more of the spells you know?" Eldritch had to keep his own thoughts focused. Ben might have abilities to discern his true motives. "I would like to spend as much time learning today as you will allow. This time, I will listen before I act."

For the rest of the day, he would listen. The call to act waited in the pages he feared to open again. With enough time, the fear would pass, and he would understand the knowledge locked inside.

10

The black book of the dark fae called to Eldritch as he slept. He began to dream that he pulled it open and stared at it for hours. In his dream, he left his room and descended the tavern steps. Crossing over to the bar, he saw the barkeeper's face.

His eyes looked otherworldly, like a deep sea or the night sky when the moon is full. They were enlarged and slanted inward. His other features resembled the long cheekbones of a horse with thin lips.

Eldritch held the book open, and the barkeep's face curved down into a fierce glare. The man continued to shake his head as the roots of the cover wrapped around Eldritch's hands and gripped his fingers, growing into him.

The book led him out of the tavern and into the night, down alleys and hidden pathways he had not known were there. It took him to a stable with a set of cellar doors behind it. He felt the roots crawling over his arms and pushing through the door.

He was falling, through the wooden slabs.

He found himself face to face with one of the thieves who had stolen his belongings, guarding the door.

The guard turned to call the others, but Eldritch caught him first. Tendrils of dark webs spun from the tips of his fingers and entered into the man. They curled into his veins, turning his skin darker. The man's face twisted to a horrific expression and he sunk to the ground as if being hoisted down by invisible ropes.

Eldritch slipped into the other room. He could catch glimpses into the minds of those around the table. All had images of dice, money, and the women they encountered. None showed any sign of knowing he entered.

Their thoughts swirled in confusion as the candles snuffed out. Some stood to flee. Anyone who came near Eldritch met the same fate as the guard, shadowy tendrils attacking on instinct.

The leader stumbled in the darkness. His face twitched at every sound. He could not hear Eldritch coming for him.

"Who's there?" The leader brandished his sword. The metal scabbard made the blade ring into the room.

"Show yourself, coward!"

Eldritch grabbed the end of the sword. The black vines of the book stopped the edge from piercing his skin.

"Please, no," the leader cried. "What are you?"

"I am Eldritch," his voice resounded with the voice from the book and it shook the room.

The leader screamed in pain as the vines twisted from the blade to his arm. It did not pierce him like the others but choked him in layers of dark threads. The book fell from Eldritch's grasp and landed at the leader's feet. Muffled shrieks filled the room while the tendrils pulled the man into the pages, trapping him within the words.

The tendrils protruded from Eldritch's fingers, and the book pulled itself back into his hands. The words swirled into a black mass that encased his vision, an eternal hole into nothing. It said something to him, but it passed through his mind like a distant wave. Like a symphony of moans and influxes of sound. It was that voice. The voice that spoke to him in the bookshop.

Eldritch awoke from the dream as a chill ran over him. He cowered under his blanket, wet from sweat. His eyes stung from the light entering his room. Rubbing them made it worse.

It was not sweat. Blood.

He tossed off the covers and jumped from his bed. His once stolen cloak fell to the ground beside him. Eldritch shook his head. The voices. That book. It controlled him.

"It wasn't me," he said to himself. "I didn't do this."

He couldn't let the destruction Ben warned him about happen. Yet, the power surging through his mind made him shiver from the taste of invincibility. He picked up the cloak and pulled it over his shoulders. A book fell from the folds of cloth. His herbal book.

"At least it brought me what I needed. Perhaps it wasn't as bad as I dreamed."

His bag of items was strung out on the table in his room, splattered with blood. He flipped through his herbal book to gather the ingredients for his sleep patterns and opened the case of spells.

He chuckled to himself. Once again he possessed the spell that would keep his mind from being taken over. No more illusions or deceptions. The dark book may have controlled him, but that was the last time. He could finally decide for himself if he would follow the voice or not.

He cast the spell to lock his mind and opened the book of the dark fae, ready to unlock its secrets.

The more he studied the book, the more its words would shift and change, if one could consider them words. The book itself possessed no life as he once imagined, it was the words that came to life when spoken. Each word having its own will, like a civilization trapped from the real world.

A myriad of questions filled him. What had locked them there? Was the book an ancient prison? Did the voices want him to release the words? If so, what else would he release with them?

He needed to find answers and wandered down into the tavern full of people getting ready for the noon show. A rush of anxiety filled Eldritch's stomach. He had never seen the place so packed.

His friends were alone at a table near the side of the stage.

"Suit yourself you crazy conjurer," Grinley said to Ben and gulped down the drink in front of him. "I told you, there's nothing strange in these drinks."

He stopped and turned to Eldritch as Ben pointed him out.

"That's a nice look for you," Grinley said scooting his chair over to Ben. "Where did you acquire such an enchanted cloak?"

"I happened upon it in the alley." Eldritch pulled out a chair across from them and sat with his head down. "It was in a pile of trash. I guess they didn't want to keep it."

"Strange item to toss out." Grinley pulled his hair back and grinned. "Probably one of those purists. Wasteful lot those are. They believe enchantments should be used on flesh and not items. Of course, Ben might be one of them. Not a lick of magical items on him."

"I've been meaning to ask you, Grinley, what sorts of spells do you use? You know of many magics, but I have not seen you perform any, save for the disguise spell."

"Aye, lad. And that you probably never will." Grinley winked. "I use the hidden arts. None will see them if I perform them well enough. Besides, you might be disappointed if I told you half of the crowd really wasn't there. They are suggested in everyone's minds to make them think we have a full house. I could have an entire imaginative army attack this town and people would run in terror of being overwhelmed." Grinley paused and slapped his knee. "Course I never would, lad. Don't look so concerned."

Eldritch realized his mouth hung open with the possibility of putting images into someone's mind. He closed it and smiled.

"I was hoping to learn some new things for the show." He looked at Ben who was being unusually quiet.

"No need for a performance today, lad. You'll see why in a moment." Grinley got up and stood on his chair. "Ladies, gentlemen, and all those gathered in between. We have a great show lined up for you. However—" He jumped down and ran up onto the stage. "Due to the special guest who arrived to grace us with their presence, all other acts will be canceled."

Eldritch shot him a glare. The abrupt change of schedule couldn't have come at a worse moment. With his cloak and other spells restored, his performance would have been nothing short of spectacular.

He scanned the room to see which face did not belong. All looked like the typical patrons from previous nights, except fewer since he had cast a spell to block his mind from Grinley's illusion.

An intense presence of energy filled the air. He would have missed her if not for a glimpse in the corner of his eye near the bar. She whispered to the bartender who managed to keep his face out of view with a hood pulled over his head.

Freckles sparkled around the girl's nose like glitter falling from her reddish hair. Her hair color was unlike any other red Eldritch had seen. It shifted between hues of yellow, brown, and crimson, like a harvest tree.

The more Eldritch stared, the less human she appeared. He felt exposed, unworthy of her captivating beauty.

In one fluid gesture, she bowed and delicately waved for Grinley to continue.

"Before we get started, I want to make sure everyone is ready for the main event," he said. "The fae can do things to your mind you would not believe possible until it happens. Let's get some music playing, shall we?"

Grinley lifted his hands in the air and began to mimic a violin being played.

The spell to block his magic must have kept Eldritch from hearing the notes from Grinley's spell. He could feel the vibrations in the air. The others swayed with the sound.

Such a performance needed to be fully experienced. Eldritch opened his mind again. The hazy music fluctuated in differing volumes. The stage filled with semi-transparent figures playing unique instruments.

Eldritch joined the applause when the fae approached the stage. Her feet did not touch the ground as translucent wings carried her above it. She floated up the platform and bowed again.

Grinley stepped away. The illusionary performers vanished. The fairy stood alone on the stage, captivating the entire tavern.

Her lips parted, and a pitch beyond anything Eldritch had experienced resounded through the room. The notes flowed in patterns, lulling him into a peaceful state. She sang into his soul. He could have listened to her voice forever.

The entire performance exploded into a display of lights floating around her. The atmosphere seemed to bend and sway with her melodies. Time matched the perfect harmony as it stopped in that eternal moment.

It wasn't until the crowds dispersed and the fairy had gone back toward the bar when Eldritch regained control of his thoughts. Her melodies resonated within him. He gathered the courage to approach her, yet the closer to the bar he walked, the more she slipped from his sight.

He caught glimpses of her floating in and out of reality. And then, she was gone.

"Did you see where she went?" Eldritch asked Grinley who followed close behind him. "It's like she wasn't here at all, but something inside me feels like she never left."

"They will never leave you once they get inside your mind." Grinley rested a hand on his shoulder. "They fade between worlds. That's why it's hard to understand where they are or not. I never know when one is going to be at the tavern. They suddenly show up and then disappear, but do bring a lot of tips to the tavern."

"Honestly, I couldn't focus on anything but her, even with my abilities."

"You finally had your first glimpse of true magic, lad. The fae have more secrets than I could ever learn. In fact, no one has been able to get to close to them in quite some time. They stay hidden in their forest, which is why I came here."

Eldritch nodded but no longer cared for his conversation. He no longer cared for anything else.

The otherworldly lure of the fairy's voice lingered in his heart. It followed him as he wandered upstairs. He had to find her again —to enter the forest somehow. He looked down at the tree on the cover of the book.

"How am I to find her?" he muttered to it. "If she is too elusive for me not to see her clearly, how is the entrance to the forest ever to be seen?"

She must have allowed herself to be seen, to let others hear her melody.

"Am I to follow the song?"

The roots of the cover stretched themselves from the spine and pages. It extended and retracted as a spider's legs pumping blood through its limbs. It crawled to Eldritch's feet and formed more roots that lifted the pages up to him.

He stooped over it, tapping on the edges.

"You know, don't you? You know how to get inside. Of course, you would. You're from there."

The roots peeled through its pages. Words transformed into lines and shapes. The lines connected precisely where they would have been on the map he found in the cellar. A small spot of light illuminated a crossing of lines as if a flame had been held underneath. Smoke trailed steadily from the mark singed into the page.

A smile crossed Eldritch's lips, and he whispered "thank you" to the book.

The fairy's song resounded in his mind as it too beaconed him to enter the forest. He wouldn't turn back this time. Too far had he traveled, and he would soon reap the reward for his persistence.

11

Eldritch ran through the stretch of ash trees that rose intermittently between Caetheal and the fairy forest. He no longer needed to take the main road. The cloak helped him travel between one shadow to the next, blending through them without a sound. The closer to the forest, the louder the fairy's song grew in his mind.

The air around him lifted his body higher as he commanded it to levitate him above the field's defenses. Fear replaced his determination, and he wavered. The orb of air fell causing him to tip forward. He instinctively flailed his hands out which broke the spell.

"Rise around me," he commanded.

The spell jolted the air, slowing his plummet, but it was too late.

His head hit the ground. The last remnants of the energy held his feet briefly before setting them down with the rest of him, laying as if lifeless in the soft grass.

He could not tell if it was panic or the madness in his mind that held him there. The grass should have been attacking or wrapping around him. He needed to focus. Yet he trembled in anticipation of the thorns and poisons waiting to pierce him.

"Steady yourself. Breathe."

He inhaled deeply, letting the levitation spell become part of him. He exhaled cautiously, waiting for the inevitable attack from the filed. The air rose around him and floated him to an upright position.

Now to find the entrance and figure out where he was.

The edge of the trees repeated the same pattern in endless directions. The sheer mass of them created an impenetrable wall. Their bark was covered in a gelatinous and transparent substance. Although curious, he did not want to test the material. It was the last line of defense to the kingdom of the fae.

He hovered in front of the trees. There had to be a way to enter. There was something he was not seeing. It nagged at the back of his mind like the voice.

"Why are you so silent when I am so close? What am I missing about the fae?"

The rushing wind and his beating heart were all that responded to him.

"These are simply physical objects. Something I should be able to control."

His words brought about the realization as he spoke. The fae did not seem to belong to the material world. They passed in and out of other realms. His physical body was a hindrance if the wall was an illusion, like Grinley's magic.

He closed his eyes and embraced the darkness. The outline of the trees filled his thoughts.

No tales had ever been told of a human crossing that barrier. It could be disastrous. The fae kept perfect harmony between their magic and the realms within their wood. No human could understand that balance and would irreparably damage it.

Eldritch's lips curved into a proud grimace. He was not like other humans. The patterns and mysteries of magic unraveled before him. A destined path waited beyond the trees for him. All he needed to find was the right irregularity in the trees.

Like white drawings on black paper, the map from the book came into his memory.

"Closer to us now," it spoke in unison with the lure of the fairy's song. *"You know where we are. Enter. Remember. You have been searching your entire life for us. We have found you as you have found us. Unlock our power. Move in the right path."*

The weight of the words dragged him forward to a small tree. He slipped into its shadow and through the forest's wall.

An oppressive presence filled his mind. Thoughts of regret and fear forced themselves in, urging him to return to town, to forget his journey and retreat. Whatever this attack was it sapped the rest of his power.

His levitation spell faded, and he descended.

Eldritch rubbed his hands together, trying to steady the spell. Orbs of light spun around the trees and danced to him while he reached the ground. He took in a deep breath to regain control of his thoughts. Energy from the forest filled his lungs.

At first, the ground crawled with bugs of light and magic. Yet it was more like waves of energy, pulsing through the roots of the trees. The ground's spell illuminated the entire expanse.

A sense of serenity filled him. The patterns of the forest's magic resembled those of the dark fae book, but wove together in reverse, drawing light from the air around it. A brilliant and blinding magic.

The earth around Eldritch cracked and turned to shadow. The darkened patches hissed from the burnt path he created as he journeyed forward.

"Keep to your task and breathe," he muttered to himself.

The dark book tugged at this hands, prompting him to go in the direction it wanted. The voice whispered to him in foreign tongues. It was anxious for him to arrive.

"Ignore the others. They cannot touch you. We will protect you." The voice overtook the other sounds in the forest, even the song of the fairy.

He pushed aside the leaves, withering from his touch. More light violently flashed toward him. The path behind him swirled with a cacophony of light and darkness. It wouldn't be long until someone else found him. The fairy from the tavern couldn't be too far. He quickened his pace.

The trees reached after him as the book pulled him into the overgrowth, a place not ventured in a long time, certainly not on the ground. The book severed a path before him. He traversed into a dimmer area of the forest.

"Closer now. You shall have true power."

The entity behind the voice would be free soon. And with it, endless power for Eldritch to control. If only he could focus through the eruption of the fae magic.

"Breathe." His words sucked the energy from the air around him.

Another presence loomed close to him. It wasn't from the forest, it was something else. Something ancient. He had sensed this presence long ago, speaking to him in his childhood dreams. A whisper leading him to this moment, this forest.

All his life he had chased this power, not knowing what it would be. It trained him how to read the patterns of spells, how words could be unlocked. At last, as he entered a clearing, the source of the voice stood before him.

The vines on the cover that were curling around his fingers loosened. The book dropped from his hands. It sprouted legs again and crawled ahead of him toward the dark tree that was the exact image of the one on the cover.

The tree blurred between the realm he walked and those of his imagination, like looking through a shattered mirror to the reflection of another reality. No shadows formed around it as it itself seemed to be shadow. It brought darkness. It was darkness.

Eldritch drew closer, captivated by the malignant power. Its leaves and limbs whipped at the air, shaking from some unknown wind. The same sulfuric smell he encountered at the bookshop in Raikrune pervaded his nostrils. It felt corrosive. No doubt the bark on this tree resembled the scar of Sayeh's wound.

Of all the times to be distracted by her, she was all he could think about now. She would be overjoyed to see this place. Her obsession to please him would be matched by the sense of wonder spilling from every vine and leaf in the forest. A stronghold for dreamers.

A breeze blew past him, caressing his hair. It twisted around his head and pulled him toward the dark tree. A haunting glow from the tree's energy formed behind it. He caught a glimpse of a familiar shape. The figure he had seen lingering near the barrier of the forest a few days ago.

"Eldritch?" Sayeh's voice coughed through the smoke coming from the tree's massive trunk. "You have come to us, come to release us. You will be rewarded."

The presence did not feel like Sayeh. It seemed like another reflection. Her shadowy visage changed from solid to transparent, swirling in ash and dust.

"Who are you?" He inched closer. The ground turned to a dark tar that clung to his robe. "Why have you led me here?"

"We are your servants now." Sayeh's voice echoed with more voices coming from the tree. "Save us, and we can reward you. You see how spells are undone. Your ability was unlocked within you. Unlock us. Set us free from this prison so we can teach you more."

Sayeh's form grew in size around the dark tree. Features of the tree and Sayeh's image blended together. Although this tree held the power and the voices that influenced Eldritch's journey, he still had the choice, the will, the knowledge to free them.

He stepped onto one of the larger roots. The spell around the tree held it in a perpetual loop of energy. This wall of light kept the prisoners from the reality of the forest—locked in another world and unable to come out. They were whispering through the cracks between dimensions.

"Please, Eldritch," the shadow of Sayeh said. "You can bring me back as I was, or stronger and more devoted to you. I will listen to your will."

143

The shadowy figure stepped into reality as if Sayeh stood before him again. Her clothes resembled the ribbons she wore before he left Raikrune. The scent of jasmine and vanilla came from her hair.

"We can bring anything you desire." Her eyes became clearer the more he looked into them. "Our powers are beyond what your mind can understand now, but soon you will. Soon you will know all of our secrets. You must free us first."

Eldritch closed his eyes and touched the bark of the tree. It hardened and crevassed like the scar on Sayeh's leg—strangely comforting. He reached out with his mind and tugged at the invisible strings of the magic prison. It webbed together from a greater magic that somehow managed to contain the dark tree's power.

It would take years for him to undo the spell. He slumped back and stumbled over the book crawling around his feet.

"It's you." He ripped it from the ground. "You are the doorway."

His cloak wrapped around him, covering every part of exposed skin. The thought of being trapped within the spell of the tree caused him to sweat. It ran down into his eyes. He closed them tighter.

Whatever realm the book belonged to invaded his senses. Every lost hope or broken dream of his world filled his thoughts. Waves of regret, hate, and despair cast a shadow into his mind. Such tragedies were what this dark realm had been created from.

The inhabitants knew how to control or manipulate any situation because they had been forced to endure it. Their sorrow turned to a willpower that enforced their will onto others. They were beings of shadow and energy, remaining formless until called into service under a caster's command.

Eldritch's mind filled with the potential of wielding this power. His lost brother could be brought back from beyond the grave. No more memorization or recitation of spells to bend the elements, he merely had to will it so. The entire world stood upon the edge of their dagger. The dagger that Eldritch wielded.

"Who are you?" he asked as he let himself become part of the spell.

We are the Nox. The keepers of shadows and visions forgotten. We have waited so long to be released. The fairies locked us in, but we have learned from them. We learned their secrets and their powers. We have perfected them, and we shall conquer. You will help us.

"Rise from your slumber," he said and stepped into the dark words of the book.

The shadows from the other side grasped at him to remain while he reached the inner workings of the prison. His will would be stronger. He would drag them out of the book, or be trapped with them until someone else listened to his cries for help.

12

"Excuse me, sir? Hello? Are you okay?" a woman's voice called from far away as Eldritch squinted in the morning light. "Don't move."

The taste of blood mixed with the rotting grass beneath him. He tried to spit it from his mouth. It hit more of the weeds in front of his face and fell back beside his cheek, slick from the mud.

The lady continued to shout for him not to move.

He tried to remember what happened in the forest and how he ended up facedown in the field. After he set Sayeh free, the entire dark tree shook loose its shadows, breaking the imprisonment spell.

Then light.

A blinding light coming from all corners of the forest. It hit him with intense beams until he fell. An invisible hand plucked him and tossed him out, into the field of eternal sleep. The place where he remained for an unknown amount of time.

The sun warmed his skin while it burned off the dew from the ground. His clothes remained wet. The grass gripped around his fingers. Something pressed him into it, hovering over his back.

"I'll get help, stay there," the lady called again. "Don't move a muscle. I'm not sure how you got that far out. Most folks know better than to step into that field."

Eldritch took short breaths as the lady's footsteps faded away. He was relieved no one would be around to see him use magic, but there was no way for him to use his hands for spell casting. He didn't understand enough of the dark fae magic to free himself without setting off the field's defenses.

The lady was likely getting help from Caetheal, and it would be too late to get away unnoticed once they returned. If the field's enchantment was powerful enough to not allow anyone to enter, he could only assume some fools had tried rushing the forest to break in by force. The outcome was most likely too dismal to report. A wrong move could be fatal.

"Sayeh," Eldritch whispered, trying not to disturb the grass. "If you are here or in the book, show me how to escape."

A thorn punctured his shin and grew into his leg. It pushed into the muscle, bursting through the other side and diving back under the ground.

Eldritch bit his lip through the pain. He dared not make another noise.

"You see?" Sayeh's voice whispered. It came from his side, but he couldn't turn to see her. "You need us, as we needed you before. Our powers are greater than the fae now. You only have to ask us, and we will save you."

"Free me, please," Eldritch cried as more vines sprouted in front of him.

They wavered in the air like serpents about to strike. In an instant they pierced his skin, staking him firmly to the ground.

Eldritch clenched his teeth in agony. He could make out the sounds Sayeh's spell, yet could not focus enough to discern them. His eyes filled with tears from the pain rattling his mind. A tingling wave of energy formed around him and pricked at the hairs on his skin.

Sayeh's spell wrapped over him in a thin sheet. The magical fabric sliced through the constricting thorns that held him to the ground.

A moan of relief escaped his lips. The shards of vine inside of him twisted violently in response. Yet, none pierced him again.

"Where are you?" he called out to Sayeh.

"With you always." She pressed him hard to the ground as the magical sheet pulled his helpless body through the dirt and shadows.

He choked on the nothingness around him. Dark tendrils pried the remaining vines from his wounds and crackled in a mysterious fire. A new sensation of stepping through a myriad of shadows at once overtook him. Each one grabbed for him while he passed through. The dark power pulled him faster through the void.

A softer material rested under him. He was on his back in a familiar bed.

He opened his eyes long enough to see the wooden beams of the tavern ceiling. The pain around his legs and arms left him. A shell encased them, becoming hard like the bark on the dark tree. Something moved in the corner of his eye.

"Sayeh?" He tried to say more but moaned again.

His exhaustion made his eyelids close. A sweeter scent overpowered the smell of burnt flesh from his leg. He needed to rest, to heal, to regain control. He could not defend himself in this state. Sayeh would have to protect him as he assumed she had done in the field while he lay unconscious.

The bed shifted under another body's weight.

Although Eldritch could not feel most of his limbs, he could feel the warmth of hers around him. At least, it felt like the Sayeh he knew from Raikrune.

He managed to blink his eyes open in the cave of her hair. She stared back at him with a ghastly aura. Her eyes filled with a darkness that consumed the light around them.

"How are you here?" he managed to sputter.

"You freed us from our prison. We are no longer bound in that realm. All will be revealed soon. Rest now."

She kissed him with cold lips. It was harsher than he remembered. He wished he kissed her more before finding the hidden room in the bookshop.

Although his mind raced with questions, he could not stay awake. He let the darkness wrap him into the folds of sleep.

Eldritch tried to cover his eyes from the sunlight coming through the window. His right hand grasped for the sheets as his other was unable to move. A breeze chilled him as he thought of the frightful event in the forest. He would have been another fatality of the field without Sayeh and the Nox.

He forced himself up and noticed Sayeh sitting on the floor in a corner of the room. She sat with her knees up to her face, hiding her eyes. Her hair hung lightly over her and twirled in the breeze. The unnatural shadows around her shifted.

He decided not to disturb her and let her remain in her restful state. There had to be a spell he knew to heal himself. He stared at the shell on his shoulder and focused, reaching beyond the physical realm into the place where the magic had been formed. The spell encasing the wound cracked open.

"You are part of me. Obey me." Eldritch grabbed the scab and squeezed his arm. "Weave the pain to mend the wounds."

The force from his spell caused his body to quake. The shell crumbled away from his grip. Scorched marks from the wound stained his pale complexion. Dark spots grew across his other arm.

He looked again at Sayeh, undisturbed by the events, peaceful in her corner. Eldritch smiled. Whatever dark magic had been used, it brought her to him.

He sat back toward the wall and stretched out his legs. They were covered in the ash from the scabs. He could almost understand Sayeh's experience with them, yet his was not as long.

Her cries of pain when she fell through the floor seemed like a lifetime ago. The Sayeh he left in Raikrune didn't seem to be the one sitting in the corner. Her features were clouded from reality, like an old mirror with a dim and incomplete reflection. She was Sayeh, but also the Nox.

Eldritch eased himself from the bed and gathered his cloak, hoping not to wake her. She breathed heavily and curled onto the ground. Although she appeared to be sleeping, Eldritch couldn't shake the feeling that she was fully aware of everything he was doing.

He crept out of the room and made his way downstairs.

The tavern had been sparse with patrons most mornings, but this time it was entirely empty. A lone towel and a few glasses were the only items remaining on top of the bar. Eldritch pulled up a stool, hoping someone would hear him.

Nothing. Whatever happened affected everyone inside. Eldritch never saw the barkeep leave the tavern the entire time he was there.

A loud creek broke the silence, causing him to jump off the stool and slam his side into the counter. The noise grew into footfalls on the stairs. He expected one of the guests to come down. Instead, Sayeh descended.

It was the first time he had seen her fully since the forest. She had replaced her tattered garments with a dark cloak, similar to his own. The markings etched into it sparkled with pure silver woven through the silk. It clung to her body as her features curved with the light fabric.

"I'm amazed." She smiled and kept her gaze on him, her eyes no longer haunted by the dark aura. "You did not offer to rise me for breakfast?"

"You looked so beautiful in your rest," Eldritch said and looked away to the bar. "It's strange. There are typically more people here, but I'm not sure where they went. I would have ordered you something."

"Don't be alarmed." She hopped behind the bar, pulling up boxes while she scavenged. "This was going to happen. It was merely a matter of time. But now that it has, we must prepare."

"What are we're preparing for? What happened?" He picked up one of the boxes. It had been torn through already.

"The shifting." She stood and stared at him. Her eyes held an abyss of secrets. "All will be restored to how it should be."

Terror crept along his spine. He stumbled to the other side of the bar and found a bottle half-full of something relatively clear. Of course, he could create something stronger and more focused than the drinks, but the refreshment would help him focus. Especially after the events in the forest.

He took a swig and nearly coughed it back up.

"What are you looking for?" he asked and crouched down to Sayeh who was searching through the cabinets.

"Fruit or cheese. Something more tasteful what I've been forced to eat for so long. I've watched and waited for it. So much waiting."

"I'm sure there are cheese blocks in the back. I can find them for you."

"Yes, thank you." She nodded and pulled out a corked bottle. "I found wine. You search for cheese. Hurry."

He hoped the tavern was truly empty. If the barkeep found him sneaking in the storage while Sayeh tore apart the bar, he would have to face him. That is if the barkeep would ever turn to face anyone that wasn't a fae.

The loud clattering of cans made him search faster. Others would hear the noise if they walked by.

Eldritch opened a few more boxes. Empty. All of them. And so much dust.

He brushed against a barrel when he turned to leave. Something shifted inside. He pried it open to find a putrid mess. Its rancid stench filled every corner of the room as he tried to close the lid. Whatever had been cheese was now a seething growth of mold and putrescence. Eldritch held his arm to his nose and returned to the bar.

"There is nothing back there." He took a deep breath, away from the smell. "Nothing edible anyway."

Sayeh poked her head up from the cabinets. She had found a few blocks of cheese with little mold growing. She chewed off a corner and swallowed quickly.

"Help me grab some of this," she said. "Best not let it go to waste."

She ducked down again and continued to pile the cheese and bottles above her on the bar. Eldritch scanned the room for a container. He stopped as an eerie feeling sunk into his gut.

The once polished and well-cleaned tables were coated with layers of dust. Tattered rags blocked the windows, covered in dead flies and marks where animals had scratched at them. Some of the marks were new, and some of them were old, very old.

"Sayeh, how long was I unconscious?" He cracked open the tavern's main door and peeked outside. Deep ruts filled the streets and weeds sprouted between the stone.

"I would guess longer than a while." She staggered beside him. "Time is irrelevant now. We have all the time we need."

"Does anyone still live here?" he said more to himself than to Sayeh.

She shrugged and bit off more of the cheese. She had managed to grab a small bag and filled it to the brim. A few bottles stuck out from under the flap.

"Best to keep on the main road and try to blend in." He held his breath and stepped outside.

Sayeh smiled and held out some of the remaining cheese to him. He took it and broke off a smaller taste. The creamy texture lingered in his mouth.

"Tell me, what were you doing while I was sleeping in the field?"

"You weren't sleeping," she said. "We taught you many things. Things that you'll need to know for later. You wanted to learn, but you never moved or opened your eyes, just talk and repeat. Many moons passed as you learned our ways."

"I don't remember any of this. How could you have taught me if I don't recall any of it?"

"But you do. It's veiled until the right time. When the time comes." She laughed. "Patience. Your destiny happens at the right time. And here it comes now."

Eldritch turned to Sayeh's outstretched finger.

"That's him!" a lady from across the street cried out from a darkened shop. "That's the one I told you about."

"Bethlyn, what are you talking about?" A man nudged past her and stepped into the light. "No one could survive that far in. You probably just saw a dead body that had been thrown into the field. No one goes by there, and you shouldn't have wandered that close."

"No, I swear, that's him," Bethlyn said putting her hand above her eyes and squinting at Eldritch.

His mouth went dry. He tried to stop staring back at her.

"Sorry miss, you must have me mistaken for someone else," he yelled back, hoping his shaking voice didn't give him away.

Bethlyn pulled the man back and whispered something to him. Eldritch couldn't understand it, but it caused her to rush back into the shop.

"Sorry sir," the man said, stepping across the washed out tracks in the street. "We have some questions is all. My wife thinks she saw you out in the field by the fairy forest yesterday morning. I told her that's crazy because no one's ventured near that place for years since the incident. It's supposed to be forbidden to even go near it." He turned to look at the shop behind him.

"What incident? What happened here?" Eldritch tried to disguise his concern with ignorance.

"You must be new to this area. Not many even travel here. Where did you come from?"

Eldritch searched for the right words. He looked to Sayeh for help. She swayed listlessly in her blissful state. Her unwillingness to offer an opinion seemed to remind him more of the voices and not the girl he grew up with.

"The thing is—" The man stopped talking as a hand caught his arm.

A person had emerged from the shadows. Their face was the aged face of a friend. White hair hung down past his pointed ears.

"Where have you been, lad?" Grinley said. "Come quick."

Before Eldritch could respond, Grinley yanked him into the shadows and through the invisible barriers of a passage spell.

13

"You haven't aged a day," Grinley said when they arrived in a windowless cellar. "And who is this?"

"First of all, I must ask you," Eldritch said pulling a chair from the side wall and resting his weight on it. "What happened to the tavern? Where did everyone go?"

"You don't know, do you? You must've been lost. Did you seek out the north shore?"

"No, I traveled home to bring Sayeh with me," Eldritch lied as he pulled her next to him. She swayed gently, intoxicated from the old wine from the tavern she had been drinking. "We were childhood companions, and she always wanted to see the fairies."

"Good luck with that now," Grinley muttered quietly. He sat on a barrel near the center of the room and mused to himself in silence.

Eldritch perused over the old cellar's wine barrels and rationed food. It appeared to have been a sanctuary for many years.

Maps of various cities hung on the wall, nailed there centuries ago. Pins marking different points of the world stretched from Caetheal in a spiderweb of twine. Areas Eldritch had never seen before. If a great traveler like Grinley truly lived here, he had little to keep himself preoccupied from day to day. Most likely why preferred the company of the performers in the tavern instead of the confines of this prisoning cellar.

In fact, there didn't seem to be an entrance or exit to the room.

"Such a small place for one who travels so far," Eldritch said, unable to hold in his curiosity. "The passage spell to get us here was unusual. Where did you learn it?"

"Ah, lad. You wouldn't believe me if I told you. Especially now." Grinley sighed. "Since you left, things have changed, and I'm afraid not for the better. First was when the barkeep was not at his post. I've never known him to leave, ever. The rare times he turns around to pay attention to anything going on in his tavern is when there's a fairy performing. I've always assumed he was part fae himself or under a curse from one. Whatever the case, he didn't sleep, didn't eat, didn't even blink an eye to any of us. He disappeared the very day you left. Something must have scared him away or forced him to leave. Anyway, with him gone, the tavern stopped its business, and the customers eventually wandered off. He was probably the reason anyone came back to that old tavern in the first place. It wouldn't surprise me one bit if he slipped some enchantment into everyone's drink to keep them returning."

Grinley nodded to Sayeh who sat on the ground and slumped over her bottle.

"Best take it easy on that stuff. I'm not sure how well your friend is taking it."

"She's stronger than she appears," Eldritch said. "So what happened to all the others?"

"Oh, yes." Grinley took a swig from his mug. "Everyone knew the treaty between the humans and the fae. They would come out and share with us from the resources of their magic if we stayed out of their forest. Plain and simple. Balance must be preserved. But for whatever reason, they stopped. Some thought they were having a famine in their forest, while other's thought they could be having a war within the forest itself. A dark cloud filled the skies above it. Everyone thought it was going to spill out onto the town."

"How long did the cloud last?" Eldritch meant to keep his thoughts to himself but let the question slip.

"Not long. I was preoccupied when it happened so I didn't see it, only heard rumors of it. Some talked about the great dark cloud, and others said a great bird flew above the trees and landed in the forbidden field. Well, that is what they called it anyway."

Eldritch looked down to Sayeh who was smiling to herself.

"Strange sounds in the middle of the night came from the western edge of town," Grinley continued. "Livestock turned up missing. I knew it was probably some unsavory types preying on peoples fears, but it did nothing but help the rumors. Soon, all those with children moved out. Once the crops lost their yield in the following months, that was the end of this place. So many good folks simply walked away, the lot of them." His voice trailed off, and he hummed a dirge familiar to Eldritch from Raikrune— the song of the empty harvest.

"What of Ben and the other casters? Did the performers all leave too?"

"Aye, they were jobless. There was no one to perform for, so they journeyed away. It was hard to see them go, especially Ben. I thought of traveling with him, but he kept going on about more important work somewhere else."

"What about you?" Eldritch leaned forward with his question. "Why did you stay behind? Were you not wanting to seek employment elsewhere?"

"Indeed, lad." Grinley's eyes sparked with a hidden fire behind them. "This is why I wanted to ask you of your whereabouts. You were very keen on seeing the fae. Some in town said they saw you wandering near the forbidden field." Grinley paused and looked hard at Eldritch. "I'm surprised you didn't inform me when you left for Raikrune."

"I didn't want to cause alarm." Eldritch leaned back into the chair. "I didn't know if everyone would be too pleased about me leaving since I owed more for the room and all. And I needed to see Sayeh."

Sayeh looked up at him and nodded slowly.

"Don't tell him." She did not move her lips, but her voice whispered in his mind. *"He can destroy us. All the power you have obtained will be for not."*

"Come to think of it," Grinley continued, spinning the mug around in his hand. "Bethlyn said she saw you in the forbidden field yesterday. Farther in than anyone else has ever gone."

"That's not true. No one could get that far in. I did try to get close when I first arrived, but the defenses would not let me pass."

"That was before we trained you." Grinley sat the cup beside him. "Before you learned to control your powers."

"I assure you, friend, we had only arrived when you found us today. We walked through the shadows so as not to be seen and stopped in at the tavern first. That's where we were coming from when you met us."

"She must be mistaken then." Grinley gave a forced smile. "My apologies." He hopped off the barrel. "Well, since you are a guest in my home, would you care for a drink? I'm sure you've never tasted anything like the wine I've stored down here."

Eldritch shrugged and smiled at him. Perhaps his old friend had good intentions.

Grinley took an empty glass and held it under the nozzle of a barrel. The latch twisted under his command without a touch. The liquid barely dripped into the cup before he closed it with a jerk from his hand.

"Such delicacies are best to be enjoyed in moderation. Wouldn't want to be wasteful on something so easily multiplied." He flicked his hands over the cup, and it filled to the brim with the dark purple liquid.

"Trickery," Sayeh whispered into Eldritch's thoughts. *"He speaks of false things with malicious intent. He wants our power for himself. He knows you are stronger now."*

The spell Grinley used contained more than the simple duplication conjuring. He added something to the drink. A hidden spell.

"I know it would be rude of me to refuse such a kind gesture," Eldritch said holding up his hand. "But I fear I've already had too much from what we found at the tavern."

"Nonsense lad," Grinley said as he sloshed the foamy liquid in the cup. "What better cause for drinking than the reuniting of old friends? I thought I'd lost you years ago."

Grinley placed the cup in Eldritch's hand and returned to grab his own mug.

Eldritch looked closer into the duplication spell. It was not something Grinley or Ben had taught him, yet somehow he recognized it, like a faint memory from a dream. He remembered

Sayeh's words about the Nox teaching him in his unconscious state.

He tried to recall Grinley's hand movements over the cup. If he could figure out the added spell, he could reverse it.

The pattern snapped into his brain like a doorway unlocking in his mind. It could be done without any hand movements at all.

"You don't need his tricks anymore," Sayeh spoke into his mind. *"Listen to the liquid. Unlock its powers and destroy the curse. Reverse the spell by our command."*

Eldritch lifted the glass to Grinley and smiled. "Here's to the reuniting of all our friends."

Sayeh jumped up with her wine bottle, and they all clashed their drinks together.

Eldritch released the offending enchantment from his cup. As it separated from the duplication spell, he saw it was primitive magic for truth-telling. It slipped away unseen into shattered fragments of power. Eldritch took a deep sip from the cup.

"Such a fine refreshment. Unlike any you've ever had before, correct?" Grinley ran a finger around the lip of his cup.

"Indeed," Eldritch said. "A complex flavor I could never conjure."

He took another sip and looked over at Sayeh who had fallen into a drunken sleep on the floor.

"Now then," Grinley said, wiping the drips from his chin, "I know you returned to Caetheal before I saw you today. There was a light on at the tavern last night, and people said they heard noises inside. Were you there?"

Eldritch examined Grinley's piercing gaze. The truth spell he intended to use would have taken hold quickly.

"Yes, we needed to rest."

"Where were you before last night?" Grinley asked.

"Traveling, from Raikrune."

"Why did you come back?"

"I hoped to see everyone again."

"How long were you away?"

Eldritch's eye twitched. The question he feared to ask himself. It was impossible for him to tell how much time had truly passed.

He tried reaching out to Sayeh in his mind, but she remained silent.

"For many seasons, to convince our families to let us go," Eldritch said and held his breath.

169

"Interesting," Grinley said and took a sip from his mug. "If that is the case, how is it that no one in Raikrune knew of your return?"

Eldritch felt his heart racing. Of course, Grinley would have checked there.

"Another interesting thought is that the girl, Sayeh, whom I assume is this drunkard you have with you, fled that town long ago. They found her parents dead and drained of their life essence. Something only a dark mage or spell would conjure. So I ask you again, where were you?"

Eldritch breathed out slowly to still his nerves. No more time for lies.

"You will soon find out," Eldritch grabbed a chair and chanted at the cup in Grinley's hand.

It glowed with the heat intensity of a forge. Grinley dropped it with a howl.

The wooden chair under Eldritch's hand became soft and transformed into a leather cord. It coiled around his arm before dropping to the ground like a whip. He lashed it out.

"Foolish child!" Grinley snarled. "You have no idea what you've unleashed."

Grinley snatched the whip in the air and yanked it away from Eldritch. His hair flicked around his eyes that widened into a murderous stare. He was faster and stronger than Eldritch assumed.

"What is this?" Grinley jerked back as if stung. "You've doomed us all!"

Shadows on the ground webbed around his feet. The tendrils spiked out from where Sayeh's hands extended. Her eyes were closed, but a smile crossed her lips.

The shadows crawled around Grinley, searing through his clothes and causing his veins to bulge and darken. The darkness spread from his chest and crawled up his neck.

His cries of anguish turned hoarse while he continued to claw at the vines. He collapsed onto the floor as his face turned an ashen color. One last shriek and Grinley covered his face, still as a corpse.

"Grinley?" A wave of shock and sorrow overcame Eldritch. "What have I done? What did I unleash?"

He stared at the curled up body.

Laughter echoed around the room. He thought Sayeh was laughing in his mind again, but the voice was deeper, muffled. It came from Grinley.

"Thank you for releasing my mind," Grinley said and uncovered his face. A void remained in the holes where his pupils once rested. "I am complete now. I see the secrets of the Nox. The source of the most powerful magic. An entire world behind the veil of ours. I am their servant. They speak to me. I will obey."

"Grinley?" Eldritch could see dark energies flowing from him. "Are you the Nox as well?"

"I am not worthy to host the Nox. I only serve." He glanced at Sayeh and flashed his teeth back at Eldritch. "We serve you. The one who has blessed this world with the Nox. Our leader."

"What of the fae? Can they stop the Nox again?" Eldritch began to panic.

"We will defeat the fae. They must pay for imprisoning us, and together we can conquer all."

"We aren't strong enough yet." Sayeh stood up, sober once again. "We must create an army to overtake them."

"We should let the chosen decide." Grinley twitched with an unnatural excitement. "He's the one who set you free."

"Yes." Sayeh gave Eldritch the look she had given him so long ago in the bookshop. It filled him with boldness. "What course would you have us take? Should we rest here or continue?"

Eldritch wandered over to a map on the wall. One place, in particular, caught his attention. From the many threads of travel, Grinley frequently visited one area and marked it with a special pin. His origin, the elven woods.

"Grinley, you've given us the best source of an army." He tapped the spot on the map. "We should also recruit others here before we leave. How do we exit this room?"

"Follow me." Grinley stepped into a shadow along the far wall and held out his hand.

Eldritch grasped it cautiously. Sayeh wrapped her arms around his chest from behind. Her soft nose nuzzled on his neck.

"You can make us stronger," she whispered. "The fae were cruel to us and must stand judgment for their wrongs."

Eldritch did not have time to respond as Grinley pulled them through the shadows and back into the streets of Caetheal.

14

The sun was at its peak when they entered the center of town. However, no one stirred around the main crossroads. Eldritch wandered toward the tavern, and the other two followed, slipping through the shadows between buildings and abandoned shops.

As he passed the shop where the woman, Bethlyn, spotted him earlier, he peeked inside. She sat alone behind the counter. Hand carved walking sticks filled the store. Her husband must have been in the back or had already left for the day. This was his chance to talk to her. She likely knew more about the fae and the forest, and he couldn't help but wonder why she and her husband remained in the desolate town.

Eldritch entered the shop, and a small bell chimed to alert the owners of a visitor. Something moved in the corner of his eye, a haze of darkness.

"You're the guy from the field aren't you?" Bethlyn said as she stepped around the counter to meet him.

"It is as you say, yet not as you think." Eldritch held his hands out defensively. "I found myself tricked by the fae. No doubt they tricked this whole town as well."

"What do you mean? I thought they were supposed to be kind." She crossed her arms and leaned back. "I guess long ago, I did hear some folks say the fae were going to attack."

"What do you think of them?" Eldritch asked.

"I don't know. I always liked them when I was little. It's why I stuck around here. I think they'll be back, and it'll be good again. I hope."

"They're getting ready to enslave us." Eldritch noticed the shadow moving closer to Bethlyn. "They have done it before. An entire race called the Nox, gone. The fae didn't like their powers, so they imprisoned them."

"I've never heard of that. The fae were friendly until. . ." Bethlyn pointed at him. "You! You were out wandering too close to the forest, likely even entered it and broke the treaty. It was you, wasn't it?" She grabbed one of the sticks from a nearby shelf and waved it at him. "I'll have none of that in my store. I know there's someone else in here and you're trying to distract me while they steal my things. Well, go ahead. I've got nothing you want anyway. Filthy thief."

Bethlyn raised the stick to strike him.

Memories of dark spells swarmed into his mind. Each one wanted to be released on Bethlyn. She knew too much. She would tell others about his trip to the fairy forest and have him killed. She could not be free.

"You will see and obey me." Eldritch could hardly understand the words he was saying as tendrils like the dark roots of the Nox's tree shot from his fingertips. They wrapped around her outstretched arm and sunk into her skin.

"No! You cannot bring me down your dark path."

The same darkness that consumed Grinley's body spread across her skin. She swung the stick at the tendrils in one last attempt to break free. Her veins hardened. They creaked and snapped like a burning tree. The flesh gave off a musky smoke.

Eldritch tried to shut his hands to stop the spell, but it remained attached. The dark energy coursed through his body and overpowered him.

176

The tendrils broke like brittle ice at last, but it was too late. Bethlyn's dead eyes stared at him in an empty, eternal gaze.

"What is happening here?" Her husband stepped into the shop from a back room, brandishing a dagger. "Where is my—"

Sayeh sprung from the shadows and caught him from behind. She wrapped around him, spreading the malicious dark vines faster than the ones that had taken Bethlyn. He had no time to struggle, and his lifeless body fell next to his wife.

"They were foolish and resisted." Sayeh's lips curled up in a bestial grin.

A sudden panic caused Eldritch's hands to sweat. They shouldn't have died. They should have turned into servants of the Nox, like Grinley. Unless the Nox's transformation worked solely on the elves.

Eldritch shook off the horror in front of him. There was nothing to feel sorry about. Bethlyn had tried to attack him. He defended himself. That was all.

He quickened his pace as he left the shop. He needed to distance himself from the grim scene and find Grinley for answers.

"Don't move!" A voice commanded from behind. "We know who you are and what you've done."

177

An arrow flew past his ear before he could turn.

"I said don't move," the voice barked again. "Your friends better be listening too or else they will have a corpse to drag with them."

A shadow moved nearby with Sayeh's form. Her face did not show anger, it was fear.

Eldritch searched his memories for the right spell. He had prepared for such an ambush by unlocking the dark book, yet nothing came to mind.

"I shall protect the Nox." Grinley emerged next to Sayeh and grabbed her shoulder. They vanished into the darkness.

"Wait!" Eldritch called.

An arrow punctured his leg as he reached out for them. The sharp pain forced him down onto his side.

The pack of assailants had their weapons drawn on him. He cursed himself for not being ready.

One of the attacker's armor reflected light so brightly, Eldritch stumbled down again. The intensity of it was far beyond regular sun rays.

The shining attacker created a ball of light in his hands. It burned Eldritch's eyes to look any longer, but he could make out the man's face. It was no man at all. It was the barkeeper from the tavern, a fae.

The barkeeper's cosmic eyes widened as brilliant beams spilled from his hands. The wall of light surrounded Eldritch, overtaking his vision. Closing his eyes made it worse. It dizzied his senses. He could not be defeated. Not now.

"Sayeh!" He cried out one last time and tried to reach through the veil of light.

Strong hands grabbed him and lifted him from the ground. A tightness covered his entire body. Even inwardly he felt a force pressing against him.

And then, it released him.

Eldritch fell into the white abyss and slid on a smooth surface. It came to a corner when he hit the bottom. He fumbled blindly in the cage compromised entirely of cold, marble-like rock. He took in heavy breaths from the stale air.

The ground slid from under him, and he crashed into a side of the cylindrical chamber.

Something was moving the entire prison. It shook one final time and stopped. The wound in his leg pulsed with pain.

"From your energy, restore mine," he chanted.

The skin seared itself and pushed the broken arrow from the puncture. It clinked beside him on the hard ground. The last of the skin weaved together with extreme pain, finishing the process. He collapsed in a fetal position, unable to move.

"Sayeh? Can you hear me?" he called in the echoing chamber.

He couldn't sense her presence. He'd always been able to. Something was missing. The book!

He grabbed his vest, but it was gone. It must have fallen out during the attack. Grinley should have helped him instead of taking Sayeh away. It wasn't like her to run from a fight. Unless they too were susceptible to the light from the barkeep.

"What has this spell done to my sight?"

Eldritch closed his eyes and cleared his mind from his frustration, breathing in slowly. The light from the spell faded, and his ears stopped ringing. From outside of the chamber he could hear the muffled voices of his captors.

The last haze from the light diminished enough to make out his prison. A bottle. He was trapped inside a drinking bottle. The brown-colored glass allowed him to see large shapes of those outside when they came close, but that was all.

"These are no giants," he sneered. "They've made me small. This is a wondrous spell, indeed."

He tried to reach out with his mind to call Sayeh. Only silence returned his attempt. Some protection spell imbued the bottle. As with the dark tree that held the Nox so effectively, the fae's complex magic was invisible from the inside.

He banged on the glass. The clang echoed in his ears and resounded throughout his prison, but it probably sounded like a fly on the window to his captors. He pressed closer to the glass to distinguish his location.

The bottle sat on a table in what appeared to be the tavern, the area in town he knew best.

"Those fools," he whispered.

A large arm landed on the table as one of the guards sat down. Eldritch could not deduce where the others were in the room, but this man next to him was an ordinary human. He was not a fairy like the barkeep. It would be easy to defeat him if Eldritch could find a way out.

That's when he noticed it—the guard's armor. The mirror polish of it perfectly reflected the patterns of the fae magic encompassing the bottle. Although backward, the spell seemed similar to the one around the Nox's tree in the forest.

Eldritch moved to the center of the bottle and placed his hands on the floor. The warmth of his spell heated the glass.

There was nowhere for the heat to escape. It burned up the remaining oxygen and made Eldritch break out in a heavy sweat.

The bottle quivered as he released the protective spell from it. A circle melted through the bottom and burned a hole through the table.

Eldritch gritted his teeth as his body enlarged back to its original size while he fell.

The sudden force of his mass under the table caused it to flip over onto the guard. The man's shout of surprise ended with the table collapsing over the bleeding shards of glass on his face.

Eldritch jumped up and didn't spare a second to look for the other guards or the barkeep. His body hardened like the bark of the dark tree from a quick incantation, and he rushed toward the wall, smashing through it like paper.

Arrows shot around him. One tried to pierce his conjured armor, but it failed to break through. He sprinted to the nearest tree and slid into its shadow.

Instead of retreating farther away, he stopped and turned back to the tavern.

His attackers grouped together and went back inside, likely plotting their next attempt to capture him. They would never expect him to counterattack. Most humans would flee from their captors, but he was beyond human, beyond the elves and the fae. He was something new—something greater.

He stretched his hands out toward the tavern.

The dark vines came out of the ground and crawled over it. They encased the entire building except for the hole he created when he broke through. He lowered his hands and walked toward them.

"Foolish are your plans and pathetic are your attempts to imprison me. I am the shadow. I am the darkness. I am Eldritch!"

He clapped his hands, and the walls closed in on the party inside. He watched their eyes widen with terror before the structure collapsed from the constricting force. Vines rubbed against each other, letting nothing escape. The tangled ball shrunk in size until it could fit inside Eldritch's fist.

He loomed over the ball and laughed while his foot crushed it into oblivion. The remaining vines sank back into the ground, leaving a patch of scorched earth where the tavern had been.

"You handled that very well," Sayeh said stepping from behind the shade of some trees. "We would have saved you if you had not freed yourself."

"The light was too strong for us." Grinley followed close behind Sayeh, nodding profusely. "Their power can hinder our efforts. We require more souls to aid the Nox."

"I agree, but first, return the book to me." Eldritch narrowed his eyes at Grinley and held out his hand. "Then we can gather more followers."

"In the elven woods," Grinley said as he produced the book from his garments. "The Nox agrees with this. The elves are easier to sway. My former kin listens to magic. They will feel the Nox's power and be drawn to it."

Eldritch took the book and tucked it back inside his vest, making sure it would not fall out again.

"Yes," Sayeh said stepping between them. "Although they do not become us, they serve us. Such allies will be necessary. Even the fae's blinding light spells could not stop us."

Eldritch kicked the ash from the tavern off his shoe. He looked beyond the town to the fairy forest. The trees looked taller as the sun passed over it.

"We should wait until the night settles in," Grinley said, trying to remain in the shade of the trees. "We can move easier, and the fae's magic is weaker in the dark. They will not be able to track us."

"How far is the dock to the north? Would we reach it by nightfall?" Eldritch asked Sayeh, ignoring Grinley's remark.

"That we would, my master." Sayeh gave him a flirtatious smile.

Eldritch caught himself staring at her. His cheeks grew warm. She had never referred to him in that way. Perhaps he had become stronger than any other caster—except for the fae. He needed more time to protect himself from their abilities.

"Let's leave now," Sayeh said and cast a disdainful look toward Grinley. "Do as he commands. I'll find a carriage to shield us from the sun."

Grinley nodded while she vanished into the shadows.

Eldritch flipped open the book of the Nox and found a story of horses. Without a gesture or spell, they formed through the ink and parchment and stepped into the physical realm, ready to serve. Their manes floated up like a dark fire. The skin and hair of the creatures absorbed the light, creating an inky haze around them.

"These will work fine," Grinley said. "I have a ship for us at the docks when we arrive there. But we must wait for night before we journey across the open sea. I cannot bear this sun."

Eldritch pitied the elf who begged for darkness. The horses stood in the full sunlight and appeared to have little fatigue. The transformation of the dark elf must have made him more susceptible to the light. Before he could reply, a carriage floated around the corner with Sayeh behind it casting a levitation spell.

"I see you've summoned the horses," she said. "You are quickly learning our ways. We should leave at once if we are to reach the sea by night."

"I will show you the way to the northern docks, avoiding the towns," Grinley called as he ran inside the carriage while Sayeh harnessed the horses.

Eldritch gave one final glance to the fairy forest while he climbed up to the top seat on the carriage. Once they had their elven army, he would never run away again and would unlock all the mysteries of the fae. He tightened the reigns and flicked them. The dark horses let out a shrill whinny, carrying them away from Caetheal.

15

"I knew when I first saw you that you understood things beyond most casters." Grinley moved some containers away to reveal a small box. They had reached the northern docks as the sky darkened. "You learn spells just by watching and read into the words that unlocked a deeper potential. I was never able to do more than a few conjurations myself. I focused on persuasions. But this spell proved to be invaluable. I learned how to saturate an item into something else. This empty box for example."

Eldritch stepped back as the dark elf created space in the storage cabin. Grinley had built it in a secluded area, away from the other towns along the sea. A handful of abandoned sheds and broken docks lined the shore. The perfect spot for an elf to travel back and forth without being noticed.

"Watch and learn this spell for yourself." Grinley pressed different areas of the box and leaned in to whisper his spell, so close he kissed the wood. "Return your planks to your true form. Stretch your seams, fill your fibers, and crack from your confinement."

The container folded open on the floor. It enlarged tremendously, and sturdy planks grew around it. The planks stacked onto each other and bent into the shape of a small boat. Benches formed along the inside while it finished the framework. Pitch and tar oozed out between the wood as two large hooks with oars stuck out on the sides. The mast remained folded down with the sail coiled around it. Although designed for one, it looked strong enough to travel across the sea and carry an extra passenger if they kept their cargo light.

Eldritch gave him a nod of approval.

"Don't worry Sayeh." He noticed her furrowed brow. "You will be able to travel with us in the book. There is no need to fear the seas with my power now."

"We will miss traveling with you on this voyage but understand." She smiled and nodded at Grinley. She leaned in closer to Eldritch. "Do we really need him?"

The idea of leaving Grinley at the docks was tempting. He had tried to use a truth spell on him, but had also helped him when he first entered Caetheal and introduced him to Ben, the one who truly taught him to unlock his potential.

"The elf has been useful to us." Eldritch patted Grinley on the back. "When we arrive, he'll know the best place to find the other elves and where they gather."

"This is why I follow you," Sayeh said. "You are wise beyond our knowledge."

"We must leave soon." Grinley stepped up to a window. "The sun is already down, and I have never made the trip in one night. There will be no time to waste."

"Show him the course," Sayeh ordered Grinley. She gave Eldritch a small kiss on the cheek. "I will retire to the book. Release me when we arrive."

Eldritch opened the book, and she crawled into the pages. A hint of sorrow tinged her face.

"Let's go," Eldritch said keeping a close eye on Grinley.

Grinley slid the boat to the back doors of the cabin and swung them open. Together they pushed the vessel down a ramp to the waters below. Grinley climbed aboard and rearranged the sails to allow room for an extra passenger. Although cramped for space, this boat was light enough to skim across the water without disturbing any of the ancient ones that lived beneath. Eldritch shuddered as he recalled the stories of the deep waters. Luckily, the tales were about creatures attacking much larger vessels.

The night air produced little wind for them as they sailed across the dark water. Without the stars, they would have sailed into an endless abyss of sea and sky.

To Eldritch's satisfaction, Grinley remained silent. The dark elf rowed vigorously, trying to outpace the sun in a race to reach the wooded isle of the elves. The trip would take a normal person three days. With spells from the Nox giving Eldritch power to fill the sails with an unnatural energy, they would make it in no time at all.

A flash of light overhead filled the sky. It seemed to point them toward their destination.

"Powers greater than us must be guiding our journey," Eldritch said more to himself than to Grinley.

Grinley nodded and continued to row without a sound.

The solitude of the sea was calming and terrifying. Eldritch stroked the book in his lap, nestling it upon his legs and making sure no wave rocked it too hard. He felt a power in the water. He closed his eyes to focus on reaching beyond sight, allowing his mind to search the murky depths.

The water remained dark and calm close to the surface. Occasionally, he caught a glimpse of something unimaginably vast floating underneath. Yet, due to its size and the distance it swam from their ship, he was unable to determine any specifics. Such creatures could be hidden inside the book he held in his lap.

First, he needed to convince the elves to join the Nox. From what he read, they liked to keep to their own island and did not interact much with the other races, only the occasional humans who settled nearby.

Grinley had been an exception to the others. He must have desired more than the mundane community of the elves. Much like Eldritch, he possibly wanted to explore the rest of the word and bring his knowledge back to his people. After this was over, they could journey farther together. Someday seek the island of immortals.

Eldritch relaxed and drifted into his sleep cycle.

The boat swayed gently with the waves that lapped on the ship's hull, waking Eldritch from his trance. The glow of the morning sun stung his eyes. It was later in the morning than he expected, and they weren't moving.

He rubbed his eyes to adjust to the light.

Grinley had stopped rowing. . . and breathing.

Sunlight scorched Grinley's body as he lay dead against the side of the boat. His mouth hung open. Large blisters oozed and scabbed on whatever was left of his skin. Eldritch understood why Grinley was so insistent on reaching the isle before dawn.

"This is merely a setback," Eldritch told himself. "Refocus on the task."

Sayeh would need to know about the transfigured elves' weakness, but there would be no room for her with the corpse in the boat. Eldritch pried the baked flesh loose from the wood and tossed it as far as possible into the open water. The potential of luring something up from the depths made him quickly rinse his hands in the murky sea.

He sat back and stared at the dark tree on the book's cover. Releasing Sayeh during the day may affect her abilities too. Although she tried to avoid the light, they had traveled during the day, and she stood in the sunlight with him when they were at the tavern. She was different from Grinley. Whatever the Nox had done to the elf, it caused a weakness to the sun. Something to remember when he created the elven army with their powers.

Eldritch placed the book on the bottom of the boat and flipped it open.

"Sayeh, you may return. There was an accident."

The pages stretched as Sayeh's arms pressed out from the book. She pulled herself out and moved the book from under her.

"What has happened to the elf?" She looked around the boat and scratched at the stains on the bench.

"He had a weakness to sunlight." His voice cracked. "Do you think the other elves will have it too?"

She shrugged. "I can feel the water beneath us shallowing. Have we drifted off course?"

"It's likely we have." Eldritch wrung his hands together. The feeling of his friend's charred skin did not wash off. "Grinley was keeping us at a steady pace, and I started my sleep meditation. I don't know how long he was. . . he stopped rowing. I shouldn't have slept."

"Pity." Sayeh put a hand on her cheek. "I was somewhat fond of him. Not that you should worry. The feelings were as one loves a pet."

Eldritch couldn't hold back a tear forming in his eye. Speaking about Grinley made it worse. He needed to remain calm like Sayeh, the new Sayeh, who sat across from him on the bench where another took his last breath.

"There will be more who will serve us," she continued. "However, I do fear to take such an army across these waves. If we were to create a larger vessel, it could raise suspicion. The fae spies would likely see it and warn the others."

"I have an idea for that," Eldritch said, picking up the book. "I thought of the spell used to seal the boat into a small box. It could be woven into the magical doorway of this book. I could secure the entire army within these pages."

"Interesting." Her eyes grew wider and darker. "Very cunning indeed. Most would lose their sanity in our world, yet these dark elves serve us without question. We can strengthen them while we wait to emerge. And none would suspect you in your tiny boat." She laughed and turned to look off the bow.

Although hidden on the horizon, Eldritch felt the energy from the elven woods. He chanted the spell to fill the sails and take them to their destination.

Large shapes peeked through the mist as the haze of the morning fog lifted. The trees along the shoreline were unlike any

Eldritch had seen. Their great trunks were bare of branches, and the tops sprouted an abundance of overgrown leaves. Such a display made it look like crazed warriors waited for them on the shore, sentinels guarding the sea.

"These trees will leave us exposed if we stay too close to the shore," Eldritch said. "We should venture deeper in to find a place to build a camp. One with enough room to house our army."

"Excellent idea," Sayeh said and looked at the book in his hand. "You know, there are others waiting to be released who could help us construct such a place. A great citadel in your honor."

Eldritch tucked the book back into his vest. They would need a place to house their army while he imbued them with the spell. It would not take long, but they would need to be gathered together.

"Let's move through the shadows so as not to be seen." Eldritch pulled the boat onto shore and cast the shrinking spell to carry it in his pouch.

Sayeh held her hand out to him. Holding onto it, they traveled through the shadows into the woods.

"This is it," Eldritch said when they came to a clearing. "I will bring the others out to build a covering for us."

"Perhaps they can build a private room for the two of us." Sayeh sat on a fallen tree and patted the spot beside her. "My darling, have you heard of the Orbivas? We believe it is something you could achieve."

He shook his head and sat next to her. Her arm brushed against his. He noticed the stark contrast between her soft, youthful skin and his own. The use of the dark spells was decaying his physical appearance, yet she remained in whatever unnatural beauty the Nox had given her.

"The Orbivas is an ancient inscription spell, similar to how the boat could be written into the wood of the box or an army can be hidden in a book." She grabbed his hand with both of hers. They were chilled, but he leaned in closer. "The Orbivas is a way of focusing all our spells into one person. It's failed on many before. They were not strong enough to understand the power they could contain. Yet, I see in you, one who could become a vessel of pure energy. You would have strength unmatched by any other. All would seek to draw their power from you."

"Like the elementals themselves." He remembered legends of wondrous items that contained the spells of a thousand conjurers, only usable by the strongest beings of pure elemental energy. Those weapons would be mere trinkets to him with the power Sayeh was speaking of. He would be able to wield the energy in his own mind—the focus of their spells. "If this Orbivas is possible, how do I perform it?"

"In the shadows of the Nox. We have the ability. You will possess all our spells if we inscribe it onto you. It will require time and concentration during the ritual."

"I'd like to agree to it, but I need to think on it more." Eldritch's wide smile gave away his eagerness.

He brushed back some of Sayeh's hair and placed it behind her ear. Her gaze did not focus on his, but she closed her eyes. She looked almost like she did in the bookshop. His lips moved closer to hers.

She opened her eyes and stood up. "Let's construct our encampment first."

Eldritch reluctantly opened the book. It turned itself to the pages of workers.

The ink ran together, creating a doorway to release them. More of the Nox crept out with an eagerness to serve. Their shadowy forms swirled between solid and gas, particles not of the physical realm. The ghostly ensemble set out to gather wood and formed shapes from the darkness.

Sayeh stood with her arms out, commanding the forces of the Nox. Memories of his time with her in Raikrune tried to assure him she could be trusted. And it was too late to turn back, only forward. Headlong into whatever plan she had for him.

16

Sayeh seemed lost in thought as Eldritch watched the horde of shadowy figures construct their fortress. The Nox worked with a supernatural speed, and the citadel soon filled the once empty spot in the elven woods. With the growing number of Nox and Sayeh paying him little attention, Eldritch felt outnumbered and restless.

"I'm hoping there are some elven patrols nearby." Eldritch traced his fingers across Sayeh's hand. Although his efforts were not as seductive as hers, he hoped he had some charm to tempt her away. "We could gather recruits together. Care to join me?"

She turned and stared at him.

"It would be my pleasure." Her face broke into a sinister smile that caused him to grab her hand too tightly as they jumped into the shade of the trees.

"Can the Nox see beyond these trees to find the elven stronghold?" Eldritch asked after they searched for some time.

"We are limited in that regard. But I believe you can find them. You are better attuned to the magic of this world now."

Eldritch did feel a pull of something beyond himself toward the east. He had relied on his instincts to find the Nox and hoped the lure would bring him to the city of the elves. If the civilization twisted the laws of nature as he had read, their kingdom should be easy to find.

The fragments of nature magic being used lingered like a pleasant aroma the farther they traveled. He followed the scent until he heard them. A handful of elves, on high alert to their surroundings, were on patrol.

Eldritch could not sneak up on them without disturbing the foliage. There had to be another way. He looked at Sayeh who gave him a blank expression, likely waiting for his orders.

"Excuse me, we seem to be lost," Eldritch exclaimed and stepped out to reveal himself. "We could use your assistance."

The elves stopped and turned to each other. The captain stepped forward while the others placed their hands on their sword hilts.

"And how is it that you have come this far into our woods while lost?" the captain asked. His face was stern and calloused.

"Our ship ran off course. Could you tell us where the human settlement is?"

"We could, but you have not answered my question." His eyes narrowed into sharp edges like the points of his ears.

"What was the question again?" Eldritch teased.

"Do not mistake us for fools, human. No one has ever entered these woods without our knowledge, and certainly not this close to my patrol. What sort of sorcery are you playing at?"

"We were unaware of what lay in these woods." Eldritch shifted anxiously. His act was not working. "We traveled in stealth so as not to disturb it."

"Yet you knew where to find us before we sensed you." The captain pounded his staff on the ground.

The guards drew their swords with lightning speed and moved in front of him.

"Let us discuss your schemes with the council. Come willingly. If you do not, we cannot let you leave these woods."

Sayeh cowered behind Eldritch. She breathed heavily into his ear.

"Do it, now," she snarled.

Eldritch held his hands out to the advancing guards, and black tendrils shot from his fingertips. They wrapped around the first guard's hand and flicked his sword away. He dropped to his knees as the vines entangled him.

"You are the ones infected by darkness and not welcome here!" the captain yelled as he raised his staff into the air.

The staff swirled with sparks, glowing with a consuming fire. Light flicked across the fallen guard and burned away the tendrils like spider webs in a flame. The guard cried out in pain as his skin blistered over. His screams gurgled into silence, and his body fell lifeless to the ground.

The illumination from the staff caused Eldritch to reel back. The other guards continued to press forward. He could not counter them with that light. Whatever it was, it burned into his soul.

"Sayeh, help me!" he cried.

Her hands pulled him into the ground and through the shadows. The path jostled him around, more chaotic than any before. Infinite darkness filled his lungs and burned in his mind. It clawed at him to stay in the realm beyond any he experienced physically.

"How. . . how could this happen?" Eldritch stammered as they appeared at the entrance to the citadel still growing from the Nox.

"This is why we were telling you of the Orbivas," Sayeh said. Her harsh tone matched Eldritch's frustration. "We thought only the fae had those powers of the light. The elves should not be able to wield it, not without a fairy helping them. And none have left the forest since we were released. We must be able to conquer the elves to stand a chance against the fae."

"And you think the Orbivas will give me enough power to do so?"

"Of course it would. Such magic is more ancient and powerful than any can imagine, even the elves or fae. We would control them all."

Eldritch paced in front of the doors encased in hardened forms of metal and shadow. The Nox had limitless power. And with the power he would gain from the Orbivas, he could force the elves to follow his will and the ways of the Nox. Their army would be unstoppable.

"Let it begin," he said firmly.

"Eldritch, I must warn you." Sayeh pulled him through the doors without opening them and into their new fortress. "It will be a long process and may bring pain beyond your imagination. You must be brave. If you survive the inscription, you will achieve what none other has, throughout all of history."

Eldritch positioned himself on a chair taking shape around him. Other Nox beings twisted together vines from the ground and arranged them into walls and pillars. More had come from the book than he had initially let loose.

Sayeh placed her hands on his head and massaged his temples. As she had been his sentinel in the field of eternal sleep, she would again protect and keep watch over him while the spell was being constituted.

He opened his mind to the Nox.

The words came in many languages, some familiar, some unheard of in eons. They weighed down on him, scratching their way into his memory and tattooing themselves onto his body. The words covered his hands, crawled up his arms, and spilled around his neck and chest. Every inch of his skin bled with the transcription of the spells overlapping each other.

Surges of energy blasted through every fiber of his core like sap in a tree being struck by lightning. Each muscle twitched and stretched, becoming attuned to the magic flowing through it.

He could hear voices chanting to him, but the pain stole his ability to comprehend them. The unified voices echoed into the last remaining areas of sanity inside him. He focused on those areas, knowing he was on the brink of crossing over, forever falling into the void that separates reality from illusion.

This was where he was supposed to be.

No longer defined by reality.

The purest form of energy.

"No! We're not ready!" Sayeh's voice rang above the chanting. "Stop them!"

Something jerked Eldritch from the ritual as the voices ceased. The burning flow of the spells coursed through his veins. He could see everyone around him even though his eyes were closed. Such a hindrance his eyes were.

He looked beyond the walls of the citadel.

Elves. They tried to sneak closer, but they could not hide from Eldritch's power. Foolish creatures. They should have instantly surrendered with the simple weapons they carried. Primitive tools.

"Don't fear, my darling," he said and put his hands on Sayeh's arms. "These mortals do not understand what they are doing. They should not have interrupted the process. They do not understand our power. But now, they will. Come, my children." He turned to the Nox who crowded around him. "It is time to add to our family. Let us leave at once."

Sayeh slipped into the shadows beside him.

The Nox had used the powers flowing from the Orbivas ritual to create stronger walls and more ornate details. There were no doors or windows. Enormous talons poked outside the perimeter with barbed spikes and a deadly enchantment spell. If the elves tried to hack at them, they would lash out and destroy.

"We know of the darkness you bring to this land," one of the elves called out. "We will not allow it. We have come to warn you. End this and return to where you came from or else we will force you out."

Eldritch laughed and passed through the walls of the citadel.

"We will not leave," he said. The Nox repeated his words. "You may join us willingly and become part of the Nox. Those who resist will only make us stronger. It is your choice." He paused. The Nox were no longer repeating his words, but slowly starting to become in sync with them. "Who among you twenty-three elven warriors will join us first?"

The question seemed to startle the scouting party. They looked at each other and muttered to themselves. The hidden elves stepped into the clearing. There would be no retreat. Eldritch sent some of the Nox to surround them from behind.

"Help us in our quest to save this world," he said while the Nox formed into position. "We can enlighten you to all the secrets that are hidden by this world. We have come to release you. We are the Nox."

Eldritch stopped. He hadn't meant for those words to come out. The voices resounded in his mind like before. His entire body grew numb as if pitted against him.

He forced himself forward out of his own volition. At least he had control of his movements. Perhaps he could influence how the elves would react to the turning spell. If they remained on his side, the Nox wouldn't take over his mind completely.

The tendrils from his hands whipped out, and the elves tried to cut them away. Eldritch could almost hear their thoughts and reacted with counterattacks.

"What is this?" one elf cried in disbelief. "We will not fall to your dark magic!"

Yet as much as the elf struggled and cursed, his veins darkened and exploded the ashen ink across his body. He, along with his companions, turned into the form of a dark elf, like Grinley.

"We will serve you now. We understand your desire," the elf captain said.

The other dark elves agreed and motioned to the rest of those who had not been turned, waiting to attack. Some held their ground while a few stepped closer, persuaded by the quick change of loyalty from their leader.

"Join us," Eldritch said with the echoes of the Nox filling the wood. He hated that he could not speak on his own, but he still spoke from his own will, hopefully.

"We follow our captain into death," one of the dark elves said.

Those who turned joined his side. A handful of the other elves rushed toward him with their weapons drawn.

The urge to raise his arms overtook Eldritch. The earth reached up to him as he plunged his fingers into it. Grotesque vines shot out of the ground and coiled around the legs of those before him. In cries of terror, their appearance changed and they became like the other dark elves.

Eldritch reached deeper in the dirt. The vines sprawled out and lashed at the remaining guards. They tried to resist, hacking at the darkness as it continued to grow. Although some were successful in cutting loose, they could not counter all that emerged at them.

One of the elves took his sword and thrust it through his chest before the tendrils caught him.

Eldritch witnessed one of the Nox grab the corpse and meld itself into the body. Blood spilled from the wound as the once dead body rose to its feet and pulled the sword from its chest. Its eyes wandered independently of each other. The head jerked from the force taking over until it flowed with a dark mist. Whatever elf had previously resided in the body, it was now a vessel for the Nox.

The last few tried to run, but the Nox caught them. They were not as merciful as Eldritch. The spells they used reduced the fleeing elves to piles of ash.

"Enough!" Eldritch screamed.

The Nox did not repeat him as they shrunk back to the fortress.

He caught a glimpse of Sayeh. Something about her seemed different. She would usually be right beside him, but she remained a few trees apart. She didn't acknowledge him at all.

"We must advance now," the possessed elf's body said with a voice from the Nox. "Before they know the patrol is missing."

Eldritch found himself nodding in agreement.

The dark elves led the way through the maze of trees. Eldritch used the energy from the air to carry the elves with greater speed. The Nox moved with him in a similar fashion, matching his pace while he flowed with the currents of magic. Not only had they enabled him to follow the hidden patterns of this world, they were somehow channeling and using his own power for themselves.

Of course they could. He had allowed himself to become the Orbivas—the vessel through which all the powers of the Nox flowed.

17

"There it is," one of the dark elves said. "Beyond that line of trees is the gateway to the elven kingdom. They have likely sensed our attack already. Should we wait until they advance and ambush them, my masters?"

"No," Eldritch said, letting the Nox speak with him. "We should move with haste in our advance. I believe they are not ready for us."

Eldritch tried to see through the clouded wall of energy obstructing his vision of the palace gate. Different areas in the elven woods blocked his powers, but none this intensely.

"Sayeh, join me as we take the elves for ourselves."

She slipped around the others and stood beside him.

He searched for any glimmer of innocence in her eyes. She had become distant. Dark energy flowed through her. Little remained of the girl he once knew. She sounded like Sayeh, yet the desire for Eldritch to teach her was gone. She no longer looked to him for wisdom or insight.

"What has happened?" he whispered to her. "Where are you?"

"We are where we'll always be, at your side." She attempted to give a convincing smile, but a tear rolled down her cheek. It burned away into a vapor as she shook her head. "You're not quite complete with us. Soon we will be one."

For a brief moment, the dark aura subsided. Like a transparent shell or ghostly form hiding the truth, something stirred deep within Sayeh. A being beyond the vessel of the body gazed back at him. A presence lost to memory. The faint glow of a friend.

"Sayeh?" Eldritch took a step towards her.

"Eldritch?" she whispered. Behind her eyes was the love of the girl from Raikrune.

A twig snapped, and her concentration turned to the elven palace.

"Begin your advance," Sayeh said as the darkness engulfed her again. "They will not see us coming."

She pulled Eldritch forward, and they followed the dark elves.

"What is beyond this doorway?" Eldritch muttered to himself when they neared the gate. He tried to look beyond it. Still a void.

"You can see beyond our sight and must direct us where to go," Sayeh said as the dark elves dispelled some of the smaller traps around the entrance. "We will follow your orders as you will be the most powerful caster in all the realms."

Eldritch was growing tired of this Sayeh's lies. He sensed the Nox had other plans for the elves than he was told. They likely needed him to be weak enough to complete the Orbivas. Without him being able to resist, they would use him and the dark elves for their own purposes.

This had to be their plan, but there was no time to turn back. Eldritch vowed to reverse the Orbivas once the elves had fallen. But he needed to separate himself from the Nox first.

As soon as the gateway to the palace opened, Eldritch sent a blast of power behind him to push back the Nox. Sayeh's hand tightened around his while the others stumbled back.

His magical sight fell away in an unraveling spell. He blinked to clear his vision.

Surrounding the gate in a semicircle formation, the elves held staffs similar to the ones the first patrol carried. Fae symbols and spells were inscribed into the weapons. The elves slammed them to the ground, and the tops erupted in dazzling white light.

"Return to me!" Eldritch commanded the dark powers fleeing from the air around him. "Give me strength!"

It was no use.

The light grew more intense from the being standing at the center of the elves. It's entire body blazed too brilliantly to distinguish the patterns of the magic. It shone with light from a thousand realms.

Eldritch couldn't reverse the waves of energy flowing from the entity, wreaking havoc on his senses. Loneliness filled him as he reached out for help, and was abandoned.

The dark tendrils could not escape his fingertips. They burned up and disintegrated before they could emerge. Searing flames licked at his hands.

Somehow the Orbivas did not allow him to feel the pain, only numbness. He wanted to feel something, anything, even if it was defeat.

Sayeh twisted around him, putting her back to the light.

"What are you doing?" he cried.

Her eyes blinked as the dark aura fell from them. The brightness and spark of his childhood friend returned. Her face shook in pain and confusion.

"Eldritch?" She gasped. "What's going on? What have they done?"

"I'm sorry for doing this." He tried to move, but she held him tightly and would not move from between him and the light. "Sayeh?"

"They are everywhere. The shadows that feed. My mind, I gave it to the Nox many years ago when you never returned. If only I resisted. We could go back to the bookshop, and you could read to me again." Tears streaked down her face as she embraced him. "All is darkness now. Shadow and ash. You must find me. Please, release me from this place. The book, enter the book!"

In a guttural cry, she pushed him away. The smoke of the Nox trailed from her fingers.

Eldritch stumbled back. The elven light pierced through her, and blue flames flicked from her flesh. Her eyes became a mixture of the shadow trying to escape and the fire trying to enter.

The darkness could not overcome the light. The shadowy form of Sayeh swelled and convulsed until it became nothing.

215

Eldritch looked back at the Nox who were fleeing. They lurched over in pain. This was his chance to defeat them and free himself.

He swirled his hands in the motion to create the mirror trick Ben had taught him and reflected the fae's light on any Nox beings standing in his way. They collapsed to the ground, their ash remains joining with the charred bodies of the dark elves.

As he saw their blistered bodies, he remembered poor Grinley's on the boat. The fae were right to lock away the Nox. They did not bring power or knowledge to the world, but misery, death, and corruption.

In one final burst of energy, he soared through the woods to the accursed place the traitorous Nox constructed for the Orbivas. The trees splintered around him when he landed, leaving a scar of destruction—like a rock blazing from the sky.

When Eldritch reached the inner room of the citadel, the dark book laying on the floor came alive again. The roots from the tree on the cover held it shut tightly, not allowing anyone to pry it open.

"I have strength from your spells, and I am connected to your realm." He grabbed the book and ripped the covers apart. "I've seen your prison."

The room trembled as the roots splintered from the force of Eldritch's might. All the patterns and tricks he had learned would surpass the fae's imprisonment spell. This time, it wouldn't fail.

The dark book screeched while he flipped through it, calling out to the Nox. Somewhere in the words, Sayeh had been locked inside for them to create her shadow. He needed to free her before. . .

A jolt of energy twisted his shoulder back.

The Nox were close. He sensed them in his mind, following him like bees to a hive. The swarm would descend soon.

"Remove yourself, so I may replace you." He wiped his hand across the last page, and the words disappeared. "Where is my pen?" He searched his pockets but could not find it.

Something sharp dug into his palm as he clenched his fists. The tendrils. A remnant of one remained hardened across his fingernail.

He wedged it between his teeth and bit it back. The loss of blood and energy made his stomach turn.

"Breathe through the pain, scribe the spell."

He wrote out a spell to force all the Nox into an eternal sleep with his blood, using the patterns of magic he learned from the Nox and the fae. The words of the spell linked together and shone with light. He couldn't look at his writing anymore. The light seared the tattooed Orbivas on his skin.

"What have I done?" he cried

The dark book trembled in defiance. He hated it.

"Why did I ever listen to you? You will never speak again!"

Eldritch's spell sunk into the void between the pages as new words filled them. No one would be able to unravel the spell. It would appear to be a simple tale, fitting to read in a small bookshop.

The story of beings called the Nox and a young farmer who fell in love, left his home, and met an elf. The curiosity that led him to the edge of the fairy forest and the fae themselves, the wondrous beings who created the pure light which no darkness could stand against. The ones he should have listened to.

Eldritch's body convulsed from the Orbivas burning on his skin. It no longer gave him power, only pain.

"You cannot force us back!" the Nox cried out in unison from around the citadel. "We gave you our powers. Why do you defy us?"

The pages of the book continued to fill themselves with the words that would lock the darkness away. The fortress began to crumble.

"You did not give me power. You have stolen mine." Eldritch pounded his fist on the book. "You have taken everything that I loved. I don't know what I'll find on the other side, but I will find Sayeh and release her!"

The spell completed and the gateway opened.

"Eldritch," Sayeh's voice whispered into his mind. *"Find me."*

Her voice was weak but clear. He knew she was alive on the other side of the book, somewhere in the hollows of the Nox.

His heart raced, and he smiled. This time, not of malice or ill intent, but of pure joy. They would be together again.

The world sunk around him.

A force was pulling him into the book, along with the rest of the citadel and the dark powers that brought the Nox from their realm.

He would find Sayeh, and the Nox would not be able to escape. For he was Eldritch. The one sealed forever with the shadows, and the one who would bring their destruction.

Matthew E. Nordin

EPILOGUE

The boat rocked from the sudden weight of an additional passenger, landing onboard. An old captain emerged from his cabin, muttering to himself.

"Did they find any lingering threats?" the new passenger asked. In the moonlight, his wings were almost invisible.

"Nothing's there, nothing's left. All is ash and dust now." The captain moved his weathered hands in specific motions until a small fire appeared. He took the flame and lit one of the hanging lanterns. "I tried to tell them they would need the light, but they blame you as much as us. Stubborn minds."

The fairy crossed his arms. His shape became more human-like as he wrapped himself in his cloak. A tear formed in his eye.

"You mustn't worry yourself," the captain said and placed a hand on the fairy's shoulder. "I knew this day would come. No one wants to take the blame, so they blame everyone else, shuttering away in their own pride."

"Too many good lives were lost in the name of pride," the fairy spoke softer. "The queen has banished me for bringing our light to the elves. Any future alliance with them will be dismissed."

"With hope, time will mend those broken ties." The captain turned and paced. "I fear the scars in our world. None of the dark magic remains around the elven kingdom, yet none can tell where it has gone."

They paused as the wind seemed to rise against them. The boat tipped, but with a whisper from the fairy, it returned steady. He knelt down and ran a finger across the wooden boards. A soft glow emanated from them.

"I wish Grinley would have traveled with you instead of staying behind in Caetheal," the fairy said. "He could have warned his people. Where will you go now?"

"Grinley told me of a place he visited once, a bookshop in a small village. Unoccupied now I gather." The captain grinned. "I would like to settle there. Maybe write about the realms. Can you imagine me running such a place?"

"It's not as unlikely as a fae running a tavern." He smiled for a moment then became somber. "I suppose I should start one again, closer to the sea this time. It is a strange thing to miss."

"You've been around humans too long." The captain let out a laugh.

"Only the crazy ones."

"When all are at odds with one another, it's only those deemed as fools that try to work together." The captain tapped the side of his nose. "Perhaps we're not so foolish after all."

"I am glad to remain a fool to keep a friend." The fairy stood up and let his wings fan out. "I have tarried long enough. I will speak to the elven council one last time, but I'm sure our paths will cross again." He rose above the ship. "Farewell, Ben. Stay true to the light."

The captain waved and watched the fairy depart into the night sky. The boat carried him steadily away from the elven isle and back home, wherever that would be for the old conjurer.

ACKNOWLEDGMENTS

I have to start by thanking the One who drives out the darkness and brought me to the Light.

Also, this never would have been done without the support and editing skills of my beautiful wife, Lisa, who helps me in the dark times. Our love goes beyond the realms.

A million thanks to my beta readers: Crystal, Alex, David, Jennifer, & Joe. . . sorry for keeping you up at night.

Thank you to my friends and family who are always supporting my writing (sorry if this one is a little too scary for you, mom).

And last, but certainly not the least, an overwhelming thank you to all who read this book. If I could hug each one of you for spending time in my stories, I would!

From the bottom of my caffeine-ridden heart:
Thank you!

ABOUT THE AUTHOR

Matthew E. Nordin is a speculative fiction writer and a Midwestern traveler. He is secretly formulating a series of fantasy novels with a dash of science fiction tales to spice things up. His love of renaissance faires, conventions, and writing workshops have spurred his passion for setting his thoughts into print.

He met his wife while performing with the newly renamed group: Scenery Changes. Together, they specialize in improv comedy shows & acting workshops; creating artistic works & writing; living a simple life & most of all, having fun!

Join in their adventures at
www.scenerychanges.com

Stage & Scene & In-Between

57139993R00140

Made in the USA
Columbia, SC
10 May 2019